The Sheridan Stage

OTHER SAGEBRUSH LARGE PRINT WESTERNS BY
LAURAN PAINE

Buckskin Buccaneer
Bags and Saddles
Guns of the Law
Six Gun Atonement
The Californios
The Catch Colt
The Guns of Summer
The Past Won't End
The Rawhiders
Valor in the Land
The Young Marauders

The Sheridan Stage

LAURAN PAINE

Sagebrush
Large Print Westerns

Library of Congress Cataloging-in-Publication Data

Paine, Lauran.
    The Sheridan stage / Lauran Paine.
        p.   cm.
    ISBN 1-57490-329-2 (lg. print : alk. paper)
    1. United States marshals—Fiction. 2. Counterfeiters—
Fiction. 3. Large type books. I. Title

PS3566.A34 S48 2001
813'.54—dc21   00-051004

Cataloguing in Publication Data is available from
the British Library and the National Library of Australia.

Sagebrush Large Print Westerns are published in the United
States and Canada by Thomas T. Beeler, Publisher, PO Box 659,
Hampton Falls, New Hampshire 03844-0659. ISBN 1-57490-329-2

Published in the United Kingdom, Eire, and the Republic of
South Africa by Isis Publishing Ltd, 7 Centremead, Osney
Mead, Oxford OX2 0ES England. ISBN 0-7531-6435-3

Published in Australia and New Zealand by Bolinda Publishing
Pty Ltd, 17 Mohr Street, Tullamarine, Victoria, Australia, 3043
ISBN 1-74030-291-5

Manufactured by Sheridan Books in Chelsea, Michigan.

The Sheridan Stage

FOUR PASSENGERS

As April ended, the rains tapered off, dazzling sunlight replaced earlier intermittent overcasts, and in different ways people and animals welcomed the advent of springtime. For cattle, it was a time of good grass, sassy-fat calves, and shedding off. For people, it was a time for admiring such things as a flawless sky of pale blue, growing things, and faint fragrances. For parents, it was a time for dosing youngsters with coal oil and blackstrap to thin the blood.

For Jack Carpenter, the burly whip who herded coaches for Great Western Stage Company, coming out of the timbered uplands and viewing the open grassland southward all the way down to Sheridan was like reexamining an old picture, at this time of year with highlights and natural beauty in all directions. He drove a willing six-horse hitch heading for the last leg of a journey that would end up in Great Western's corralyard, where there would be dry dust for animals to roll in, a bait of grain, sweet meadow hay, and a long rest.

He had one final stop to make at the stone-trough turnout seven miles above town. After that, a straight haul to the edge of town, supper, a few drinks at Morton's saloon, and a bed in the bunkhouse built against the palisaded back-alley wall of the corralyard.

The turnout was on the east side of the roadbed shaded by unkempt old pines and red firs. When the sap was running, it was a pleasant, fragrant place to allow passengers to stretch their legs while he watered the horses, which he did with two collapsible canvas buckets, because he did not like taking the animals off the pole every time he watered them. To the horses it made no difference. To Jack Carpenter it made a lot of difference. He wasn't lazy; he was simply not fond of doing something it wasn't necessary to do. After eleven years of driving for Great Western, Jack was not only senior whip, he was also widely experienced. That included making judgments of passengers as well as of his harness animates and the condition of his stagecoaches.

On this particular trip Jack had four passengers, one woman and three men. One of his passengers was a nutbrown, lean rangeman whose saddle was in the boot. Jack had categorized him as an itinerant hired hand. He hauled dozens of them every springtime.

The other two male passengers were drummers. Each had one carpetbag of personal belongings and two large sample cases. Jack rarely made a trip, barring in the depth of winter, when he did not have at least one traveling peddler aboard.

The female passenger was stocky, with eyes as blue as cornflowers, short curly hair, and a determined cast of jaw. She was, in Jack Carpenter's opinion, as pretty as a speckled bird—and young, possibly in her early twenties.

Jack was a married man with three children down in Bordenton, which was his home, but none of that interfered with his admiration of the very attractive woman passenger. While watering the stock at the stone trough, he watched his passengers stroll among the trees, stretch cramped muscles, and, in the rangeman's case, smoke a cigarette. The drummers ganged together to discuss their trade and the new, springtime items they were offering along the route, and to tell dirty stories that were also part of their stock-in-trade.

The handsome woman smiled at Jack as she opened her purse for a handkerchief, which she moistened in the trough to wash her hands and face. He smiled back—and froze. Clearly visible in her wide-open purse was an ivory-handled, elegantly nickel-plated double-action Lightning Colt with the initials E.D. engraved on the pistol's back strap.

Women who carried side arms, particularly when traveling, were not exactly a novelty, but in Jack Carpenter's years of driving, while he had seen many weapons in purses, even in muffs during winter, they had been almost exclusively derringer types, small, easily concealable weapons with very short barrels. The "E. D." Colt revolver was a full-fledged six-shooter, and it had the customary shootist's long barrel.

When the trip was resumed on down to Sheridan, Jack's habit of killing time by speculating about passengers had been dealt a hard blow. He still thought the woman with the very blue eyes and short curly hair was one of the most handsome he had ever hauled, but his enthusiasm had been dampened by that gun in her purse.

He was still trying to reconcile the woman's wonderful smile and flawless features with that gun when he wheeled up into the Sheridan corralyard, set the binders, tossed the lines to a waiting yardman, and began climbing down from his high seat.

The passengers were alighting. The pair of drummers were already striding toward the roadway when Jack was met by wizened Silas Browning, the Sheridan manager for Great Western, who met every incoming stage for information about the coaches, horses, harness, even road conditions and the weather. Jack watched the

3

rangeman sling his saddle over a shoulder and leave the yard. The handsome woman was up ahead of the cowboy, carrying her carpetbag and purse as though they were weightless. She turned left on the plank walk, heading in the direction of the Sheridan Hotel, which was the local rooming house. He was unaware of along silence until Silas made his sniffing sound of irritation and said, "You're a married man. Besides, she's young enough to be your daughter. I said there's grease on the hub and felloes of the off-side forewheel."

Jack looked down at the much older, faded-eyed, unsmiling man. He had noticed that grease up at the water-trough turnout. "Yeah. Needs a new leather."

Silas Browning sniffed again. "Anything else?"

"No."

The old man walked away to make a circle of the unhitched coach, lips pursed, eyes squinted. He was not fond of drivers, and he was even less fond of yardmen. The difference was that he fired yardmen regularly, and would have done the same with whips if they hadn't been almost impossible to replace. The world was full of wagon drivers; experienced stagecoach drivers were hard to find. Exceptionally good ones like Jack Carpenter were as rare as chicken teeth.

Old Silas finished his scrutiny of the coach and started across the yard toward his office. He saw Jack Carpenter crossing the road in the direction of Rusty Morton's saloon and made his disapproving sniffing sound. They drank. That was another thing he could not abide in his drivers, but it also happened to be something else he could do nothing about. It was as consistent with whips that they drank as it was with hard-shell Baptists like Silas Browning that they rarely touched liquor and had to force themselves to be civil to those who dispensed it.

4

Morton's saloon had a faded sign nailed over the spindle doors that said DROVER'S REST SALOON. Morton had bought the business with the sign up there. He had never liked it, but neither had he ever disliked it enough to climb up there and take it down.

When Jack reached the bar, Rusty was chewing a cigar that had lost its fire a half hour earlier. He had just served those two drummers, and was drying glasses he'd left to soak overnight in a large bucket two-thirds full of greasy water behind the bar. He stuffed the towel in his waistband, winked at Jack and went after a bottle with a jolt glass. As he placed them on the bar, he said, "You goin' to try an' make it down to Bordenton tonight?"

Jack was leveling up the little glass as he shook his head. "No. I'll ride down in the morning like a passenger. My wife's not expecting me until tomorrow, anyway." Jack paused to tilt his head and drop the whiskey straight down. He refilled the jolt glass with a stone-steady hand and jerked his head sideways. In a lowered voice he said, "I brought those peddlers down from San Luis." His hand nearly hid the little glass, which he did not lift as he eyed Rusty Morton, who was, as usual, wearing one of his elegant and expensive brocaded vests. "An' a lady you'd wake up thinkin' about twenty years from now."

Rusty's slatey eyes showed faint irony. "You might. I got broke to lead on womenfolk long ago" He leaned on the counter. Business was slack. It usually was this time of day. It would improve along toward evening. "You know that Mexican yardman over yonder, the one with the pockmarked face?"

Jack knew him. He was about the only yardman in the corralyard that Carpenter knew of who had always been

5

obliging and cheerful. "Yeah. Herb. His name was Hermenengildo or something like that that no one could say. What about him?"

"Silas fired him this morning."

Carpenter's knuckles whitened around the whiskey glass. "Why?"

Rusty sighed before replying. "All I know is that he come in here for one drink before leaving town. All he said was that it made him sad to leave because he liked Sheridan and the folks he knew here. I asked him why he'd leave an' he told me Silas had fired him right after choretime this morning."

Jack downed his second drink, pushed the little glass away, and fumbled through several pockets before finding his pretty well gnawed-down plug of molasses cured. Rusty watched him worry off a corner and tongue it up into his cheek. Rusty knew Jack Carpenter, had known him for about ten years. He leaned and waited, and when the cud was in place, Carpenter pushed upright off the counter and said, "Someday, Rusty . . . Someday he's goin' to take out his bellyaches on the wrong person."

Morton agreed, but with a saloonkeeper's cynicism. "I expect so. An' even if it's like the preacher says about vengeance bein' mine saith the Lord, an' I will repay, seems to me by the time the Lord gets around to doin' anything, bastards like old Silas would have made life miserable for an awful lot of human beings."

Jack Carpenter ponied up two silver coins for what he'd taken from Rusty's bottle, and went down to the cafe, and again he arrived in a business establishment that was nearly empty. It was too late for breakfast and too early for dinner.

The cafeman was a surly individual who could make

6

baking-powder biscuits lighter than feathers, coffee from fresh-ground beans every day, and apple pie the equal of anything any female ever baked. Otherwise he might not have lasted as long as he had.

Carpenter ate like a horse and left the cafe without more than ten words passing between himself and the cafeman. He stood out front in overhang shade sucking his teeth while watching roadway and sidewalk traffic. Directly across from him a top buggy was parked in front of the doctor's place, which probably meant Henry Pohl was patching up a kid with a busted arm from falling out of a tree or maybe examining a rancher's wife pregnant as a bloated toad.

Dr. Pohl was a newcomer, by Sheridan standards, anyway. He had only set up shop two years earlier. He had a handsome wife who served as his nurse. Henry Pohl, himself, was an inch or two below average height, was built like an oak barrel, and, so it was rumored, could unbend a mule shoe with his hands. Jack had never gone to him, had never had reason to, but he had heard two judgments, one good, one not so good, about Dr. Pohl.

He moved into tree shade to get a fresh cud into his face before striking out on an angling course across the road northward in the direction of the corralyard. It was a little early for bedding down, but the southbound left Sheridan before sunup and he intended to be aboard it, so getting a few extra hours of rest was a good idea.

There was no one in the yard when he passed the old log gates. His coach had been wheeled away and parked. On his right was the back door into Silas Browning's office; elsewhere there were horse stalls, and on the north side corrals and several little utility sheds.

7

The bunkhouse was in the northwest corner of the yard where a frugal planner had been able to utilize both the west wall and the north wall as integral parts of the bunkhouse.

Carpenter went back there, interrupted a poker game, waved the men aside, and felt for a bunk that still had decent rope springs beneath it and that did not have someone's gear lying on it.

The sun was still up, although because there were no windows in the bunkhouse and the door was closed so no light could enter from that direction, it could just as easily have been sunset when Carpenter got settled for sleep.

A NEW DAY

JACK CARPENTER AND THE DAWN STAGE WERE already several miles below town in the direction of Bordenton by the time the surly man's cafe window was steamed up and his counter was full of noisy customers, the same ones who arrived regularly at meal times: single men, widowers, an occasional stranger or two, such as the pair of drummers Jack had brought into town yesterday, and an occasional rangeman. Every springtime brought itinerant rangemen in search of work. Mostly, they lingered long enough not to be hired, then left town, but some got hired. Springtime was a busy period for stockmen.

It was also a busy time for freighters and merchants, such as Hank Dennis, the somewhat overweight, large man who owned the Sheridan Mercantile Company, the only general store for forty miles in any direction. He was out on the loading dock hand signaling a freighter who was backing his high-sided rig to the dock. The freighter had three pairs of Spanish mules on the pole. They worked so well Hank's hand signals were hardly required.

When Hank braced as the tailgate bumped his dock, a congenial voice spoke behind him. "If Silas had seen that, he'd do his damnedest to hire the freighter."

Dennis turned, recognized the town marshal, Joe Fogarty, and after nodding turned back to help the freighter unchain his tailgate so the unloading could begin. As he walked back to where the marshal was standing, his eyebrows went up a notch. "You already had breakfast?"

Fogarty was watching the bearded freighter and his swamper climb into the wagon to begin passing boxes and bundles toward the dock when he answered. "Yeah. Long ago."

They returned to the store's dark, cavernlike interior with its odor of oiled wooden flooring and halted near the crackling iron stove. Early though it was, there were already customers, mostly women with net shopping bags, but there was also a rough-looking cowman beating off dust at the counter as Hank Dennis's elderly clerk adjusted his glasses to read the list the rancher had given him. Standing slightly apart were two men with handsome, little curly-brimmed bowler hats, city suits complete with vests and neckties, and elegant button shoes. Each man had a large valise. Hank Dennis sighed about those two. "Some things a man can expect every spring: weeds and drummers. Excuse me, Joe."

Fogarty watched briefly, then strolled back out front. The roadway traffic was light, but that would change as time passed. Sheridan was the only source of supplies for quite a few miles. It was also the only place around where people could get specialized services, such as corrective shoeing, saddle and harness repairing, and doctoring.

As yet the sun had not cleared the easterly rooftops, so even the trees that irregularly lined Main Street were in shade. The chill was still noticeable, too, as Marshal Fogarty strolled to the opposite plank walk where the jailhouse stood. When sunlight came it would strike the front of the structures on the west side first. Even so, Joe kindled a fire in his office. The jailhouse was made of logs, which was a blessing when the full heat of summer arrived, but until then he had to build a fire every blessed morning.

Those thick logs had other attributes. They absorbed moisture, and they muted sounds. Fogarty did not hear the gunshot. He might not have heard it even if he'd left the roadway door open, because the bank was on the opposite side of the road and northward, south of Morton's saloon and next door to the cafe. The first he knew there had been a gunshot in the vicinity of the bank was when lanky and badly weathered Hugh Pepperdine, the saddle and harness maker, poked his head in and said, "You asleep? There was shootin' up at the bank."

Pepperdine's head disappeared as Marshal Fogarty looked around, blinked, then lunged for the door. Others had heard the gunshot, but no one was in sight up in the vicinity of the bank building, although every recessed doorway had at least one person in it peeking out.

Fogarty crossed over to the front of the general store before starting northward with a thrusting stride. He had freed the tie-down over his holstered Colt by the time he was passing the cafe, and a grizzled man with pale eyes and gingery hair stepped out and said, "Where's his horse?"

10

Fogarty did not slacken his pace as he said, "Whose horse?"

"Whoever's in there robbin' the bank," the grizzled man said, then he also started moving. "Around back in the alley. I'll go out there." The grizzled man disappeared between two buildings, scurried down the dogtrot, and emerged into the alley. There was no horse tied back there.

The only person Fogarty saw northward was Rusty Morton. He was standing under the wooden overhang in front of his saloon with a shotgun in both hands. Opposite the saloon at the saddle and harness works, Hugh Pepperdine was emerging from his place of business buckling an old shell belt and holstered Colt around his tucked-up middle.

Hugh called a warning to the lawman. "No one's come out, Joe. Don't go in there, he might be waiting."

Marshal Fogarty'd had no intention of backgrounding himself with morning sunlight by walking through the bank's front door. He halted beside it to listen, heard nothing, looked up and down the roadway, which was suddenly empty, then drew his handgun and cocked it as he called out, "Pete? You all right in there?"

Only an echo came back.

Fogarty motioned for Rusty Morton to come closer with his scattergun. He did not gesture for the harnessmaker to cross the road, but Pepperdine came, anyway. Otherwise, although by now there were onlookers behind every window as well as in every doorway, only Morton and Pepperdine were moving.

Time seemed to be standing still. When the saloonman stopped, he was north of the bank doorway. Pepperdine angled so as to step up onto the plank walk near the town marshal. Fogarty called again.

"Pete! Who's in there? Who fired that shot?"

This time there was a reply—in a woman's voice. It was so unexpected that Morton's shotgun sagged as his eyes widened and Hugh Pepperdine made an audible sigh, then turned to stare at Joe Fogarty. The lawman's poised six-gun tipped back a little when the woman said, "He's hurt. Someone go for a doctor."

She appeared in the doorway clutching a voluminous cloth purse, face ashen, blue eyes wide with shock. She was a sturdily built woman with short curly hair. Fogarty lowered his weapon and eased off the hammer as he spoke quietly to her. "Lady, come over here. Get away from the door."

She did not appear to have heard him. "Get a doctor, please. Someone . . ."

Rusty Morton hung the shotgun in the bend of one arm and walked directly over to lead the woman back northward with him. She did not resist his guiding hand. To the men who were close enough to study her, she seemed dazed.

Joe Fogarty asked a question. "Lady, who's in there? Was it a holdup?"

She turned slowly to gaze down where Fogarty and Hugh were standing. "I . . . don't know. I was waiting for the clerk. The man sitting at the desk farther back was leaning over some papers on his desk. Someone shot him."

"Is he still in there, lady? The man who shot him?"

Her eyes were fixed on Fogarty's shirtfront, where the badge shone pewter-dull by daylight. She seemed to be barely wagging her head as she answered. "I didn't see anyone. There was just the man at the desk. Then the gunshot." Her eyes rose to Joe's face. "I don't know. I'd like to sit down."

12

Rusty took her arm again, turned with her in the direction of his saloon, and as he led her past the spindle doors, Pepperdine edged past Marshal Fogarty, got as close as possible to the edge of the doorway, removed his hat, very quickly leaned to look in, and just as swiftly jerked back. He said, "Once more," in a whisper, took down a deep breath, and made his second lunge forward and back. "Pete's sprawled on his desk. If there's anyone else in there, he's down somewhere hiding."

Fogarty shouldered past and walked into the bank with his handgun moving from side to side. Nothing happened. He stood perfectly still. The acrid aroma of burnt gunpowder was strong. There was no sound and no movement. Behind the elegantly scrolled metalwork of the clerk's niche, the man lying facedown on his desk was visible.

Pepperdine came inside and stood with thumbs hooked in his shell belt looking around. Not a word passed between them as Marshal Fogarty passed inside the low woodwork that divided the interior of the room from the outer area.

He saw the blood before he reached the desk and put up his six-gun in order to have both hands free as he gently raised the swarthy, facedown man. From beyond the railing, Hugh said he would go find Dr. Pohl, and nearly collided with Rusty at the doorway. Pepperdine jerked his head and kept on walking. As Rusty was passing through the little ornamental gate in the wooden divider, someone behind the storeroom door began rattling the latch.

Two cocked weapons were pointing in the direction of the back wall as the door opened and that grizzled man with the gingery hair walked through. He saw the guns aimed at him, saw the man slumped back in a chair at the desk with blood down the front of him, and said dryly, "No horse out back, Marshal. No tracks of anyone leavin' the bank by the back door."

Fogarty leathered his gun and turned back to the man who had been shot. He was Pete Donner, head of the Sheridan Bank and Trust Company, a swarthy man with black hair and eyes, a bloodless slit of a mouth, and an ingrained expression of mistrust and suspicion. Donner had been christened Pierre Donnier. He had been born on the ship bringing his emigrant parents from France. Pete was not a widely admired individual, but, as Fogarty told Rusty Morton, what appeared to be attempted murder was against the law no matter who the victim was. When Henry Pohl arrived breathlessly behind Hugh Pepperdine, Fogarty was satisfied that the banker was dead, but he completely forgot everything else when Dr. Pohl raised quizzical eyes after examining the banker and said, "One of you boys fetch the stretcher from my office. Tell my wife I sent you for it. Now then, the other two of you help me place him flat out on his back on the floor."

Rusty lingered until Dr. Pohl was on his knees beside the unconscious man, then left to get back to the badly shaken, very handsome woman who was sitting where he had left her in the saloon.

Joe Fogarty went over to where the man with gingery hair was standing, silent, motionless, and with no particular expression, and said, "James, how about tire tracks in the alley? Maybe he left in a buggy."

The grizzled man raised pale eyes. "There are wagon-tire marks back there. Quite a variety of them, but no shod-horse marks and no buggy-tire marks."

The grizzled man was James McGregor, Sheridan's

14

only gunsmith. He was a dour man, taciturn, about average in height, with a granite jaw and a powerful build. He was a widower, a blunt man, and a close friend of Hugh Pepperdine, who was his opposite in most things, particularly tobacco. McGregor did not use it and Pepperdine chewed.

When the harnessmaker returned with the stretcher, people were ganged up out front like sheep. He had to plow through them to reach the doorway, where he halted and looked around. Two men of noticeable heft caught his attention. One was Reg Lee, the liveryman; the other was Jim Young, the tanner, whose place of business at the northernmost edge of town on the east side was alleged by many to be the source of Sheridan's inundation by blue-tailed flies. Hugh growled at them and jerked his head. They were to help pack Pete Donner down to Henry Pohl's place.

McGregor barred the roadway door until Donner had been carried away, and even then was reluctant to step aside until Marshal Fogarty produced a set of keys he'd taken from Donner, ordered the little crowd to step back, and locked the door from the inside.

McGregor went close to the blood-spattered desk and stood with both hands clasped behind his back for a while, then he joined Marshal Fogarty in examining the entire large, shadowy room.

They found nothing. McGregor thought out loud. "Looks to me like he shot from the doorway, Joe. Stepped in, aimed, and fired from the doorway and—where was Donner's clerk? Not here. Don't seem like he's been here. He could have shot him, Joe."

Fogarty had already examined the place where the clerk in his green eyeshade sat on a high stool most of the time and either accepted deposits or handed out money. He agreed with the gunsmith. "He could have, James, an' if he didn't shoot him, then whoever did could have already been hiding in here and could have run out afterward, because he sure as hell wasn't here when I got inside."

McGregor reiterated what he'd said earlier. "Not by the back alley, Joe. Unless he had wings. I tell you, there's no sign back there of anyone leavin' the bank in a hurry."

Fogarty went to a bench and sat down, gazing dispassionately at the older man. "The shootin' wasn't at real close range, James. No powder burns, no scorched cloth. But what I'd like to know most of all is: If it was a holdup, why didn't he force Pete to open the safe before shooting him?"

"Maybe he tried, and when Pete refused, he got mad and shot him."

Marshal Fogarty continued to regard the older man, but a trifle wryly now. "Pete wouldn't let himself get killed over what's in that safe. He told me that a dozen times."

McGregor flapped his arms in exasperation. "Well, now, when there's gunfire in a bank, it's reasonable to expect a robbery to be takin' place. Why he botched this robbery we're never goin' to know unless you find him, Joe. Suppose we call out the town possemen and have 'em ride out a ways and scout around."

Fogarty snapped up to his feet as someone fiercely rattled the locked roadway door. He unlocked it and moved clear as Rusty Morton walked in. The saloonman blinked. The sun was brilliantly shining outside. "I took the lady up to the hotel," he said. "She has a room there. As near as I could figure out from what she said, her name is Elizabeth Dunning, she's from up in Montana

16

somewhere, an' is on her way down to some border town with one of them damned Spanish names you can't make sense out of, to stay with a widowed aunt. She figured to leave town on the morning coach, but was just too tired to even wake up until after the early stage had already gone."

McGregor fixed Rusty with his dispassionate gaze as he said, "That's interestin'. But it don't tell us anything. She had to have seen something, Rusty. F'gawd's sake, man, she was the only one in here when Donner got shot. She had to have seen at least the muzzle blast. She should have seen the man, too."

Morton scowled. "Well, she didn't. She didn't see anythin' or even know somethin' was goin' on until the gun went off. Then all she seen was Pete slump over bleedin' like a stuck hog . . . James, she's a real refined lady. Somethin' like that just about numbed her plumb to the bone."

ONE DAY LATER

SPECULATION RAN WILD. THE FACT THAT PETE DONNER could never have won a popularity contest was almost lost sight of. In fact, there were people who before the shooting had nothing favorable to say about the banker but who, after the shooting were outraged that the town banker was sitting there at his desk, minding his own, and the bank's, business, when someone upped and shot him for no reason. It was a damned outrage.

That the vault had not been forced open added to local indignation. It was not unheard of that bankers and their clerks were killed during a robbery, but this time, according to saloon, pool hall, and cafe gossip, there

17

had been no attempt to force the vault.

The general conclusion was that whoever had tried to kill Donner had not been a bank robber, but more likely some disgruntled son of a bitch who had been refused a loan.

Marshal Fogarty heard it all during the course of the day following the shooting without being too impressed by any of it.

He went up to the hotel to talk to the only other person in the bank at the time of the shooting besides the victim, and on the way met Dr. Pohl, who said that Pete Donner was hanging on and that was about all he could say. But he was cautiously hopeful. "Most of them die in the night. Usually somewhere between midnight and about three in the morning." Henry paused, then said, "It went clean through him, nicked the lung, broke a rib, and came out a little lower than where it entered. All that blood came up into his throat and down the front of him from his chest."

Marshal Fogarty continued on up to the hotel and found the handsome woman packing. She told him she had bought passage on the southbound evening stage. He sat in the chair she motioned him to, held his hat in his lap, and made about the same assessment Jack Carpenter had made: She was something a man would remember for a long time.

He asked why she had been at the bank. Her answer was short. "I wanted to cash a voucher. I was getting low on money."

"And did the clerk cash it, ma'am?"

"No one was in the bank except Mr. Donner, but I didn't know that was his name until later."

"Did he cash it, ma'am?"

She went to the window and was leaning there when

18

she answered. "He didn't get the chance. I'd just entered, and was looking around. The only person I saw was Mr. Donner at his desk. I was about to speak to him when the gunshot nearly deafened me."

"Did it come from behind you? Maybe from back by the roadway door?"

She hesitated before answering. "I'm not sure where it came from, Marshal. It was very loud. I was too startled. It was so totally unexpected. I was unable to move, even to think, until I heard you calling from the roadway."

"You didn't see a muzzle blast, gun smoke, some kind of movement?"

"Marshal, I just said, I was too completely astonished." She moved away from the window. "It was a terrible thing to see. I didn't sleep very well last night . . . There was so much blood. I've never seen a man killed before."

Fogarty stood up. "Your name is Elizabeth . . . ?"

"Durning. Elizabeth Durning."

"From Montana?"

She turned to face him when she replied. "Yes. From a place called Timberline. I'm going down to a border town named Pueblo de Guadalupe. My aunt and uncle lived down there. My uncle died last month. I want to be with my aunt for a while. She is the only family I have left."

Marshal Fogarty was sympathetic. "I'm sorry about your uncle."

She showed a wan little smile. "Thank you. I wish I could help you more, but as I've said, it happened so fast and so unexpectedly . . . "

Marshal Fogarty was at the door before he said, "He wasn't killed, Miss Durning. He may die, but so far he's hanging on." Fogarty smiled at her. "If he'll just hang

19

on for another day or two and get sound enough so I can ask him if he saw the gunman, it'll sure be a help. Ma'am, have a good trip."

Because he closed the door after himself, Fogarty did not see the color drain from Elizabeth Durning's face as she stared after him.

Pete Donner's clerk was an aging wisp of a man with very thin hair, a receding chin, and watery eyes that appeared larger than they were through the thick-lensed glasses he wore. His name was Benjamin Thompson, and he had been wandering aimlessly around town before Joe Fogarty found him at Morton's bar.

He did not give Fogarty a chance to ask the one question Fogarty had in mind. As soon as the marshal settled at the bar, Thompson turned and said, "I was sick yesterday. I still got it, whatever it is. Some sort of coughin' illness. I stayed in the house, kept the stove fired up, and drank lemon-watered whiskey to bring on a sweat."

Rusty brought Fogarty a glass of warm beer and walked away. Fogarty pulled the glass toward himself but did not raise it. "Did Pete know you wouldn't be at the bank yesterday?"

Thompson was removing his glasses to mop at his eyes with a blue bandanna when he replied. "Yes. I told him night before last I was coming down with something, and thought I'd better stay inside and keep warm until it passed."

Fogarty drank, put the glass down, and leaned on the counter gazing at Rusty's impressive array of bottles along the back bar. Thompson, like the handsome woman at the hotel, was turning out to be as useless as teats on a man. Fogarty downed what remained of his beer, paid up, and departed.

He walked up to McGregor's gun shop, took James back with him to the bank, unlocked the door, walked in, and was immediately struck by a lingering scent of gunpowder. He took McGregor over to the banker's sticky desk, lighted a lamp, and set it where he could see the chair. McGregor pointed to a puncture in the chair back. "I didn't see that yesterday. The bullet went plumb through him, Marshal."

Fogarty did not comment. He turned the chair, looking for an exit hole. There was none. He straightened up, digging for his clap-knife. McGregor was appalled as Fogarty slashed into the leather, tore it aside, and dug deeper through a mass of horsehair padding, and exposed a length of solid oak that constituted the upright support of the chair back. When Fogarty straightened up out of the way, McGregor let his breath escape in a hiss. It was his turn to raise a thick-bladed knife and start carving. Not a word passed between them as pieces of hard oak fell to the floor.

Fogarty held the lamp so McGregor could see better, and when they could both see the embedded bullet, James paused just for a moment, as though confirming something in his mind, then went back to work.

They ruined the chair back, and the floor was littered with shavings, horsehair, and pieces of leather, but they got the bullet out. McGregor placed it atop the desk where Fogarty put the lamp, stood scowling downward for a moment. When Fogarty said "Well?" the gunsmith finally raised his pale eyes. "It didn't come from a forty-four or a forty-five, Marshal. I'll have to take it back to the shop and sort of size it before I can be sure, but right now, if you want a guess, I'd say it came from a smaller-calibered gun. Maybe a double-action gun. Want a guess?"

"Yes."

"From a Lightning Colt. From just lookin' at that bullet right now I can just about take an oath it didn't come from anything of a larger caliber."

When they left the bank, McGregor had the bullet. Fogarty said he'd come up later and see what James had figured out. He went down to the general store for a sack of tobacco and stepped back to allow one of those traveling salesmen to depart. The man nodded genially and hurried on past.

Inside, Hank Dennis was examining some clippings of bolt goods with his glasses on. He rarely wore glasses, and had to remove them to identify the marshal coming toward him. He always acted a little self-conscious when someone caught him wearing spectacles, as he did now when he abruptly folded them and put them out of sight below the counter, then covered this up by offering a piece of cloth to Marshal Fogarty. "What d'you think? Will womenfolk want to make dresses out of it? I bought three bolts. It was a good price, an' feel that stuff, Joe. Now that is quality goods. Ought to wear like iron."

Fogarty examined the piece of cloth. It was dusty blue with tiny blossoms like filigree blooms all over it. "It'd make a real elegant shirt, Hank."

Dennis's eyes showed a spasm of irritation. "It's not shirting."

"I need a sack of tobacco and some wheatstraw papers," Fogarty said, putting the piece of cloth down.

As the merchant was turning away, he gestured. "Look at those guns I bought off that other drummer. Brand new. The latest in the Colt's Patent line."

Fogarty walked over to the glass-enclosed gun case. There were six shiny new weapons among the other

22

handguns, which had been in the display case long enough to have lost the sheen from their bluing.

Dennis brought over the tobacco and papers. Fogarty paid him while standing in front of the glass case. When that transaction had been completed, the portly storekeeper went behind the case and removed two of the new guns. When Fogarty stood with his hands at his sides regarding them, Hank said, "Hold one, Joe. Balance it. They're a hell of an improvement over that four pounds of iron you're carrying."

Fogarty made no move to touch the guns. He said, "What's the name of the drummer you bought them from, Hank?"

"Name? William something-or-other. William Booker. He hired a room for overnight at the hotel. He's leaving town on the evening stage. Why? You can't buy one any cheaper from him than I'll let you have one for."

Fogarty raised his gaze from the guns to the merchant's face. "Forty-one-caliber Lightning Colts, Hank."

"That's right. Go ahead, heft one."

Fogarty still didn't pick up one of the weapons. "Did this peddler demonstrate one of them for you?"

"Yes. An' he sure can handle a pistol. If he can shoot as well as he can twirl a gun and draw it, I'd say he's in the wrong business." Dennis laughed. "He could make a lot more money robbing trains or something like that."

Marshal Fogarty said, "Obliged for the tobacco," and left Hank Dennis standing there looking puzzled as the marshal walked out of the store.

He was having a cup of coffee at the jailhouse office when Jim Young walked in. Despite the tanner's best efforts, no amount of scrubbing or changed clothing ever completely dispelled the unpleasant odor that went with his occupation. He left the roadway door open, which may have been an oversight but more likely was a trait he had developed over the years when other people opened doors and even windows when he was in the same room with them. Young was a large, well-built man with taffy hair and small blue eyes that smiled a lot. He neither smoked nor drank. He was a Mormon. He was a hard worker, and while he was not brilliant, neither was he stupid. Just a little dense.

He waited until the marshal waved toward a chair before sitting down. He smiled as he said, "Some of us around town been wonderin' when the bank'll open. Maybe Mr. Dennis don't have to worry; he's likely got enough cash hid out somewhere to carry him over, but me'n most of the other businessmen in town ain't fixed like that. Me, well, I got a shipment of freight coming. Maybe in the next three or four days. I got to pay cash on the barrel head, Marshal. Can't do it unless I can get some of my money out of the bank."

It had not occurred to Joe Fogarty that such a situation might arise, mainly because he had not thought of the bank at all except as the place where a man had been shot. "I'll talk to Donner's clerk. He's been sick, but maybe he's well enough now to open up in the morning."

The tanner's smile remained. "I already talked to him. He said he could open the bank tomorrow if you was agreeable." Young stood up. He was a powerfully put-together individual. "It'd sure make things easier, Marshal."

Fogarty nodded and smiled back. "I'll see to it, Jim. It never crossed my mind. "

"Sure. I know. Mr. Donner gettin' shot and all. Did you know Reg Lee went out on a scout with some of the

24

town possemen this morning?"

Fogarty hadn't known. He arose as he replied, "No, I hadn't heard. I'll go look him up."

Young nodded from the doorway. "He's real good at readin' sign. If that bushwhacker left tracks, Reg'll find them."

Fogarty finished his coffee before leaving the office, and when he was out in the sunshine again he did not go all the way down to the lower end of town where the livery barn and public corrals were. He went over to the saloon, looked in, pulled back, and recrossed the roadway to walk northward in the direction of the hotel.

He was beginning to have a bad feeling about the Donner shooting. Part of it included having that peddler who sold double-action Colts leave Sheridan on the evening coach. He could not think of a single excuse for making the drummer lie over.

He encountered the other traveling man up there. His name was Ernest Macy. He carried a rather extensive line. Except for gaudy imitation jewelry, it was exclusively dress goods in bolt lots, ladies' shoes, and some very fragile-looking but elegant parasols. He told Fogarty he rarely showed the parasols unless he was in a town larger than Sheridan.

He was a genial, pleasant man of slightly less than average height. His hair was very dark, as were his eyes. He offered to show him his samples, but Fogarty was looking for the other one, the man named William Booker.

All Macy knew was that Booker had a line that covered hardware, buggy and wagon wheels, blacksmith's supplies and weapons, and that he was headquartered over in Idaho somewhere and was on the road from April until October every year.

25

What Macy did not know was the whereabouts of Booker at this time, and that was what Fogarty wanted to know.

THINGS THAT DON'T FIT

HUGH PEPPERDINE HAD CLOSED THE SHOP EARLY, AND was over at McGregor's gun shop drinking coffee with his old friend when Marshal Fogarty arrived. He and Pepperdine exchanged a nod. McGregor brought the bullet they'd dug out of Donner's chair to his counter and stood it on end. "Forty-one caliber," he stated. "Most likely from a Lightning Colt."

Fogarty picked up the slug, hefted it, and dropped it into a shirt pocket as Hugh Pepperdine, who knew the story of the bullet from McGregor, made a remark that brought Joe Fogarty around facing him.

"A man don't see too many of those guns. Lots of folks got them, I expect, but excludin' a cowboy who come into the shop this afternoon to have a torn billet fixed on his saddle, I haven't seen very many folks carryin' them."

"Who was the cowboy?" Fogarty asked.

Hugh shrugged wide shoulders. "He didn't say who he was, an' I didn't ask. He paid cash. It took me about an hour to repair his outfit. All he said was that a horse had taken to him and the billet tore under the strain. Well, he did say somethin' else, but I wasn't payin' very much attention. Whoever originally put on that damned billet had sewed it instead of lacing it. It was a mite hard to get off." Hugh paused briefly. "He said he come to town on a southbound stage with two drummers and a woman passenger he'd been hopin' to see ever since, only he figures she's gone by now."

Fogarty fished out his makings and went to work rolling a smoke. "What about his gun, Hugh?"

"Oh, yeah, the gun. It was one of those Lightnin' Colts."

Fogarty lit up, gazed at the taller and older man, then swung his gaze to the roadway window. "Did he say anythin' else about the good-lookin' woman?"

"No, not much. Just that she'd been on his mind since they both left the coach down here. Yeah, an' that she had short curly hair and eyes as blue as cornflowers."

Fogarty turned back. James McGregor was staring at him. It did not require much intuition to guess McGregor's thoughts, but what James didn't know was that another of those passengers not only carried a Lightning Colt, he also peddled them.

Now Marshal Fogarty had two people off the same stage who owned Lightning Colts. He asked Hugh if he knew where the cowboy was working, and Hugh nodded his head.

"Hired on with Reg Lee down at the livery barn."

Marshal Fogarty did not make it down there until the following day, because Henry Pohl was waiting for him over at the jailhouse. Pete Donner had a high fever. Dr. Pohl was sure he could not last another day, let alone another night. The reason he had looked up the town marshal was that Donner was delirious part of the time, and during those periods he said a lot of things, most of which made no sense to Henry Pohl, but he thought Joe Fogarty might want to see if questions would get through to Pete and elicit answers.

Fogarty nodded thoughtfully. He would try some questions. Henry went to the door to depart as he said, "My wife's got a woman hired to keep buckets of cold water handy. They're doing everything they can to bring the fever down. I don't know what it is, Joe. My guess is an infection, but except for the fever, there's no sign of one. His wounds are draining well; there is no pus . . . " Dr. Pohl shook his head on his way out.

By the time Marshal Fogarty had finished supper, dusk was settling. By the time he got up to the Pohl's combination residence and medical facility, it was nearly dark. There were lights along Main Street. At Dr. Pohl's place almost every window reflected light.

Henry's buxom, handsome wife admitted the marshal. She looked exhausted, her usually immaculate hair straggled, and there were faint but discernible bluish shadows below her eyes. But she greeted him warmly and smiled as he walked in pulling off his hat.

Henry came into the anteroom in shirtsleeves, drying his hands on a small towel. His wife left them alone. Fogarty raised his eyebrows and Dr. Pohl stuffed the little towel into his waistband as he said, "Still with us. It's hard to say, but I think they've brought the fever down a little. At least he sleeps now. Off and on."

"Is he still talking?"

"Not nearly as much. Come along."

The small room with its brass bedstead and Spartan furnishings had a wet floor, wet blankets on the bed where the wounded man was lying, and the appearance of a place where some unusual but hard-fought battle had been waged. Joe stepped around a water bucket with several soaked rags draped around it as he approached the bed.

Dr. Pohl stood back, busy with the small towel again. "You can waken him," he told the marshal.

Fogarty leaned to place a hand gently upon the banker's shoulder. Donner did not move. The gentle

28

hand went over to his forehead, which was warmer than it should have been, as Fogarty very carefully moved the head from side to side. Donner still did not move.

Fogarty stepped back and looked up with a frown. Henry Pohl moved in, held the little towel in one hand, and placed the fingers of his other hand on the side of Pete Donner's neck. After a moment he removed the hand, frowned at his patient, and said, "He's alive. In fact, that's the best pulse he's had since they brought him in here. Joe, I'm sorry I got you up here, but I think we'd better leave him alone now. Let him sleep. He needs that very much. Sleep without nightmares. Maybe tomorrow . . . Tell you what I'll do. If he speaks again, disjointed as the words are, I'll have my wife sit in here with him and write them down. I'm sorry I wasted your time."

Out on the porch Henry apologized again, and Joe Fogarty smiled at him. "You're tryin' to keep him breathing. That's more important than something he might say when he's out of his head. See you tomorrow. Good night."

He strolled slowly southward to make his final round of the town before heading for the hotel and his bed. He was disappointed; sure as hell Pete had seen the person who had shot him, and it was reasonable to think that a man facing death by gunfire would have something vividly imprinted in his mind about that.

As he was preparing for bed, he thought of something else. If, as Henry had suggested, the daylong battle to lower Pete's fever had succeeded, even partly, Pete would be alive tomorrow, and with any luck his fever would be broken, which could mean that he would survive and in time would be rational.

Fogarty was settling against the pillow when he

29

sighed. He might hear from Pete exactly what had happened at the bank and who had shot him, but if it had been Elizabeth Durning, the drummer named Booker, or some transient cowboy who worked down at Lee's barn, at least two of them, Elizabeth Durning and the gun salesman named Booker, would be long gone.

He had thought long and hard about locking them both in a cell. The problem was that according to law he'd have to charge them with a crime, and in order to do that he'd have to be in possession of valid evidence that one or the other of them had committed a crime. Right now all he had was a suspicion, and even that was pretty damned weak.

He awakened from a troubled sleep while the sky was still dark. A thought was waiting when he opened his eyes. It had not been an attempted bank robbery. Whoever had shot Donner had planned it so well that no one had seen him in the bank when he shot. Anyone that savvy would have forced the vault open first, if robbing the damned bank had been his purpose.

With a frayed towel draped over his shoulder and a bar of brown soap in one hand, Fogarty trudged out back to the washhouse to shave and scrub. The air was chilly, the sky was pocked by more tiny blinking white lights than a man could have counted in two lifetimes, and, by gawd, whoever had shot Pete Donner had done that purposefully, like any other kind of deliberate bushwhack. It had been an attempted assassination, not an attempted bank robbery.

By the time he got down to the cafe, where only three or four other diners were at the counter, he was so deep in thought that the cafeman had to growl at him twice before he looked up.

"I said, ham'n eggs'n coffee, or maybe a breakfast

30

steak with spuds an' coffee."

Fogarty settled for the ham and eggs as a lean, nut-brown man walked in wearing a face still puffy from sleep. He sat at the counter beside Marshal Fogarty, gave his order of steak and potatoes for breakfast, and rubbed his eyes. When their glances met, the lean man said, "A woman I come close to marryin' one time told me I'd ought to settle down and get me a store, then I wouldn't have to sit up all night mindin' someone's damned animals."

Fogarty considered the man. He was in his late twenties or early thirties, had the general appearance of a range rider, and did not pack an extra ounce of weight. Fogarty leaned back slowly and looked down. The man's worn old shell belt and holster were on the right side. The weapon was a Lightning Colt.

Fogarty waited until his meal had been placed in front of him and the cafeman had departed before saying. "Do you work for Reg Lee?"

The lean man nodded while reaching for the cup of black coffee the cafeman had left for him. "Yeah. Hired on couple days back when I come to town. I never worked in a livery barn before, an' I sure as hell never worked as nighthawk in one. It's hard to stay awake when all your life you been workin' in daylight an' sleepin' after dark."

Fogarty ate in silence for a while. When the nighthawk's breakfast arrived he did the same. Several more men drifted in. There was a little ripple of conversation. Not as much as there would have been if this had been the midday meal. Bachelors, widowers, men who arose very early and for whatever reason were not fed where they bedded down, as a rule behaved like bears who had been denned up all winter and had just

31

emerged into daylight. They grunted at the cafeman for food and grunted at one another by way of greetings. Otherwise they sat hunched and preoccupied.

Fogarty finished, paid up, and returned to the roadway to roll his first quirley of the day, as he leaned against an overhang upright, waiting.

When the nighthawk emerged, Marshal Fogarty turned slightly. "Feel any better?" he asked.

The lean man smiled. "Yeah, a little."

"Mind tellin' me your name? I kind of like to know who's in town."

"Don't mind at all, Marshal. Charley Wright."

The marshal genially eyed Charley Wright's hip holster. "I've seen a few of those newfangled double-action Colts, but haven't seen many men carrying them."

Charley Wright brushed the customized stock of his gun. "Well, they're a lot lighter to pack, Marshal. An' they shoot faster. Not like your gun. This here one—all you got to do is keep pullin' the trigger. You don't have to cock the hammer each time. Makes it faster." Wright made a little wry smile. "It's an improvement, but for me, it's the lightness of the thing. I've never had to shoot real fast. Hope to hell I never do."

Fogarty said, "The ones I've seen had different handles."

Charley Wright knew about that, too. "Yeah. They come with a parrot-beak grip. This here one . . . I won it in a poker session while I was winter-feedin' cattle with some other fellers up in Wyoming. I don't know who had it made over so's it'd have the same kind of grip your gun has. I just won it, rolled it in my bedroll, and that was that. I don't even recall much about the feller I won it from. I think his name was Smithers, or

Smothers, somethin' like that. You want to look at it, Marshal?"

Fogarty shook his head. "No. I just haven't seen many of them is all."

Charley Wright's pale eyes rested on Fogarty, his expression relaxed and genial. "If you hear of a ridin' job I'd sure be obliged, Marshal. I don't mind the dunging out, nor saddlin' horses for other people, but this stayin' awake all night . . ." Charley Wright smiled and walked away.

Fogarty stepped on his cigarette and crossed to the jailhouse. When he walked in, he got a surprise. That peddler named William Booker who had sold those Lightning Colts to Hank Dennis across the road was sitting on a tipped-backed chair reading a limp newspaper. He looked up, smiled, folded the paper, and put it away as he rocked forward and said, "Good morning, Marshal. My name's Bill Booker. A man named Macy who also put up at the hotel told me you might be lookin' for me."

Fogarty masked his surprise by walking slowly around to the desk and sitting down as he tossed his hat aside. "Not exactly lookin' for you, Mr. Booker, but interested in those double-action guns you sold over at the general store."

Booker was a fairly large man, solidly put up with dark hair and eyes that complemented a somewhat sallow, faintly tan complexion. He offered Fogarty a cigar, lit one himself, and returned the declined one to a pocket of his pearl-gray suit with matching bowler hat and button shoes. He looked prosperous enough.

"I can't sell you one, Marshal. Not after I sold Mr. Dennis half a dozen. My company's got a rule that once I sell something to a merchant in a town like Sheridan, I

33

can't sell single items to folks in the same town." William Booker removed his cigar, trickled smoke, and gazed at the lawman. He smiled a little apologetically.

Fogarty smiled back. "You ever been in Sheridan before?" he asked, and got back a birdlike quick nod.

"Several times. But I wasn't carrying the line of firearms back then. I was mostly carrying general hardware and smithing items."

Fogarty arose to go see if the coffeepot was full. It was better than half full, but as he leaned to poke kindling into the little iron stove, William Booker said, "Not for me, Marshal, I can't drink coffee. Got a little murmur to my heart, and doctors have told me to stay away from coffee."

Fogarty turned, watched strong blue smoke drifting ceilingward from Booker's cigar, smiled to himself, and returned to the chair as he said, "I thought you and Mr. Macy would have left town on the morning coach."

Booker tipped ash before replying. "As a matter of fact, that was our intention. We been traveling together since we come together up in Cheyenne—now there's a town a man can rack up sales in." He plugged the stogie back between his teeth. "Mr. Macy come down with a bad rash and asked me to lay over a day or two and sort of look after him."

Fogarty's eyes narrowed imperceptibly. He was ready to mention that Sheridan had a competent physician, changed his mind, and said, "I'm sorry to hear that. Sometimes around town this time of year folks get ragweed itch."

Booker stood up as he replied to that. "That might be it. I'll see if they got a salve over at the general store."

While Fogarty was seeing his visitor out, he said innocently, "That ragweed itch can make folks pretty

34

miserable. Did he come down with it yesterday?"

William Booker was dusting the fire end off his stogie when he replied, "Yes. I guess he first noticed it yesterday morning." Booker carefully put the half-smoked cigar in a coat pocket, nodded, and walked across the road toward Dennis's store, leaving Marshal Fogarty leaning in doorway shade watching his progress.

Fogarty had talked to the drummer named Macy yesterday afternoon. If he'd had ragweed itch or some other bothersome problem, he had neither mentioned it nor acted like it.

The marshal glanced southward. The liveryman was sitting in tree shade in front of his barn. He walked down there to ask if Lee had made any interesting discoveries on his scout the previous day.

A MATTER OF GUNS

REG LEE WAS A CANADIAN BY BIRTH, BUT HAD LEFT Canada at an early age and had reached his middle years by doing many things, including range riding, mustanging, and trading. He saw Marshal Fogarty approaching and tipped down his chair to arise. When they met and Fogarty mentioned hearing that Reg had scouted beyond town, the liveryman nodded. "Yeah. I didn't know what I was lookin' for. In fact, Joe, that was an excuse to straddle a good horse and go out an' listen to the grass grow. I been waitin' a long time for spring an' summer."

Lee motioned toward a little bench as he sat down again. When Fogarty straddled the bench, the liveryman sighed. "You get restless this time of year? I do."

Fogarty cocked his head as a mule brayed out back somewhere. The liveryman treated that unusual sound indifferently. "Don't mind him. You know how they are, they get real attached to a horse, an' when the horse goes away they bray an' walk the corral fence an' fret themselves into a sweat until the horse comes back. I sent his mare out on a light buggy this morning." Reg paused to squint into space. "A lady hired it. Joe, we don't get 'em in Sheridan that look like her very often. Maybe never."

Fogarty had been just a listener up to now. He straightened up slightly on the bench, gazing at the liveryman. "Husky woman, Reg? Short curly hair and eyes as blue as cornflowers?"

Reg turned his head. "By gawd, you saw her, too, eh?"

Marshal Fogarty killed another ten minutes with the liveryman, then hiked directly up to the corralyard, where the gnome who ran the place shook his head as he said, "Nope. There wasn't no passengers on the southbound last night or this morning. Just some light freight."

Fogarty crossed to Morton's saloon for a quiet beer and barely noticed Rusty's brocaded vest. It showed more color than a peacock. Another time he would have been dazzled. Around town people were amused by Morton's collection of expensive and very elegant brocaded vests. When the beer arrived, Fogarty knew he was expected to admire the vest, so he did, but his mind was elsewhere.

Four people had arrived in Sheridan two days back, and all but one, the rangeman, had business elsewhere and should have left town the morning after their arrival on the southbound stagecoach, and not a one of them had done it.

36

Fogarty thumped for a refill, and while Rusty was drawing it, he twisted to look blankly out the roadway window where sunshine reflected off roadway dust. Two of those strangers owned Lightning Colts. Pete Donner had been bushwhacked while sitting quietly at his desk by that kind of a gun.

Morton set up the refilled glass and called a greeting to a burly man with a pair of smoke-tanned gray stagedriver's gauntlets folded neatly over his shell belt who had just entered.

The burly man grinned at Morton, settled in beside the marshal, and called for a jolt of whiskey. Then he faced half around, eyed Fogarty thoughtfully for a moment before saying, "I come up early from home to look you up, Joe. Somethin's been botherin' me since I heard about Mr. Donner gettin' shot."

Fogarty waited. He knew Jack Carpenter, had known him for years. He was known as the best whip who had ever driven for Great Western. He was also known as an individual who rarely missed an opportunity to get lightly oiled when he was in town, but Fogarty had yet to see Carpenter really drunk.

"Couple days back I come through with the southbound coach," he said, pausing only to accept his whiskey from Rusty, drop it straight down, and blow a ragged breath. "There was a lady passenger." He shook his head when Rusty offered to refill the little glass. "She was somethin' right out of a picture book, Marshal."

Fogarty sighed. "Yeah. Blue eyes, curly hair, and put together like a Durham heifer."

Carpenter stood with his mouth open. He'd been about to launch into his own description. He let go a long breath before speaking again. "You saw her, too, eh?"

37

"What about her, Jack?"

"Well, when I stopped up at the turnout above town to water up and check things, she come over to the trough to rinse dust off, and when she opened her purse to take out a handkerchief, I saw a nickel-plated double-action Colt pistol in there. Not no sawed-off belly gun, mind you, but a regular six-gun with a regulation barrel."

Fogarty faced his beer glass, raised it, drained it and pushed it away, then fished around for his makings and without a word went to work manufacturing a smoke. When he was ready to fire up, he said, "Lightning Colt?"

"Yeah."

"Are you real sure of that, Jack?"

"Sure as I am that I'm standin' here right this minute."

Fogarty got the quirley lit, shook his head when Rusty asked if he wanted another refill, and leaned down on the counter. "Nickel-plated, eh?"

Carpenter answered strongly again. "Nickel-plated!" Carpenter seemed to feel the lawman's long silence was an invitation to speak. "It was none of my business an' all. Then I heard about Mr. Donner. I'm not sayin' she had anythin' to do with that, you understand. But it's been naggin' at me, so I come up early today to ask you a question: What caliber bullet was Mr. Donner shot with?"

Fogarty eyed his cigarette before replying, then what he said was evasive. "It went through him into a piece of solid oak in the back of the chair. Smashed it like a mushroom, Jack."

Carpenter tugged the gloves from under his belt and was pulling them on as he said, "Yeah. Well, I got the evening northbound, so I'd better get over there. Just worried about that, is all. See you gents on the way back."

Fogarty also left the saloon, but Carpenter had crossed the road on a northerly angle and Joe Fogarty crossed over and turned directly south and did not halt until he was back in front of the livery barn again.

Reg was out back sluicing off a stud-necked big seal-brown mare who had sweat stains on her from light harness. When Fogarty leaned in shade watching, Lee paused with the sponge and bucket to say, "You missed her by fifteen minutes, Joe," and went back to his chore.

Fogarty had not seen her on his way to the lower end of town. "Where did she go?" he asked, and got a leer as the liveryman replied, "Walked right up toward the hotel on the same side of the road as your office."

Fogarty spat aside. "Naw. Where did she go with the buggy?"

Reg waited to answer until he had upended the bucket to finish washing the big mare. "I didn't ask, an' she didn't say. She paid me, was real nice, commented about what a beautiful day it is, and walked away." Reg put the bucket aside, untied the big mare, and led her into a corral with stringers that had been cribbed so badly they would no longer support a man's weight. As he was latching the gate, he said, "Maybe she'll settle in town. That'd inspire a man to shave now an' then, maybe use the barber's bathhouse now an' then. Even buy a white shirt."

Joe Fogarty eyed the liveryman skeptically, then went trudging up the back alley in the direction of his jailhouse. There had been four passengers on Carpenter's stage who were passing through, and although there had been southbound stages since they'd

39

arrived in Sheridan, not a damned one of them had left town.

He entered the jailhouse from out back, aimed his hat for a rack of antlers, missed, and let the hat lie where it had fallen as he sank down at his desk.

Not only hadn't those four travelers departed, but three of them owned Lightning Colts, the kind of weapon the banker had been shot with.

He went over to the cafe, ate, crossed diagonally to Henry Pohl's place, and was met at the door by the physician's statuesque wife. She looked fresh and rested as she let him in and smiled broadly as she pointed to the closed door of Pete Donner's room.

"We broke the fever, Marshal. He slept well last night, and this morning when he was restless Henry gave him something to make him sleep."

The marshal looked back from the closed door. "He is asleep now?"

"Like a stone. Oh, Henry told me you wanted to ask him some questions. I'm sorry, Marshal. But he should awaken this afternoon."

"By any chance did he talk in his sleep? Has he said anything like he did when he was out of his head?"

"No. Not that I know of. I was completely exhausted last night and went straight to bed when it seemed the fever was breaking."

Fogarty thanked the woman, let himself out, and as he was walking toward the little picket gate in the fence that lined the front of Dr. Pohl's property, he put on his hat, paused to glance down through town, then turned up toward the hotel.

He did not meet the handsome woman, although he had no trouble locating her room and stood a long while knocking on the door. He even tried to open it, but it was latched from the inside. He had to assume she slept like a log, but there was also another possibility, one he worried about as he returned to the front porch, where a flowering bush of some kind with lavender flowers almost entirely cut off the view to the west. The fragrance was almost overpowering as he walked over there, left the porch, and looked down the side of the building to the window that was in the west wall of the handsome woman's room.

He abandoned the idea of peering into the window. He'd never peeked in a window in his life. The idea did not appeal to him even though he very much wanted to talk to Elizabeth Duming. He was satisfied about one thing: The window was closed, so in all probability she had not locked the door inside the house, then climbed out the window, which meant that she really did sleep like a log.

He returned to the jailhouse, made a pot of coffee, and barely heard roadway traffic as he leaned back at his desk fitting some pieces that seemed more like tangents into some kind of pattern.

He put the little slug McGregor had forced back into at least a semblance of its original shape upon the desk and stared at it.

The only one of those four strangers who did not own a Lightning Colt was the somewhat swarthy man named Ernest Macy.

He snatched up the bullet, dropped it into a drawer, and got a cup of coffee.

The bushwhacker did not have to be one of those three strangers who owned the kind of weapon Donner had been shot with.

Right offhand he could not recall seeing anyone else around town carrying one of those little guns, but

Hank's store'd had them on display in the gun case before Hank had bought the new ones from William Booker.

Nor were townspeople with sufficient reason to kill Pete Donner immune from suspicion. The bushwhacker could have been anyone, even some cowman or rider from beyond town.

Fogarty finished the coffee, retrieved his hat from the floor, and went over to the general store. Hank's clerk with the black sleeve protectors was waiting on a woman over at the bolt-goods department, and Hank was taking advantage of the midday lull to wear his glasses as he totaled a long line of figures written in a distinct but cramped style. He removed the glasses the moment Marshal Fogarty approached. He also swept the rather long piece of paper out of sight.

He waited with raised eyebrows as Fogarty walked up, leaned on the counter, and spoke very softly as he said, "Who have you sold Lightning Colts to around town, Hank?"

"Only sold one. About a year ago Pete Donner bought one. Told me he'd feel better havin' one around up at the bank."

Fogarty gazed steadily at the storekeeper. He had never seen the banker carrying a gun. If he had not taken the thing home with him, then it should be somewhere at the bank.

Fogarty went up there. Donner's clerk, the frail individual who wore a green eyeshade even on rainy and overcast days, was perched on his high stool behind a wicket of elegant iron scrollwork, counting out greenbacks for Rusty Morton, who already had stacks of coins on his side of the counter.

When Rusty turned and saw the lawman standing

there, he winked, grinned, and walked out into the sun-bright roadway.

The clerk looked inquiringly at Marshal Fogarty. Behind him, Donner's desk had been scrubbed, his demolished chair was gone, and where blood had stained the floor behind the desk someone had arranged a little parlor carpet. Everything in the bank looked as it usually looked, except for that rug and Pete Donner's absence.

Marshal Fogarty asked the clerk about a handgun and got back a wary look. "There's a derringer inside the safe, and Mr. Donner put a sawed-off shotgun just inside the storeroom behind the door."

"That's all?"

"Yes, sir. At least that's all I know about."

Fogarty considered the distant desk with its drawers. "There is supposed to be a Lightning Colt, too," he said, and entered the enclosed area to approach Donner's desk, where, under the wide-eyed stare of the clerk, he went through every drawer.

There was no gun.

CONTRADICTIONS

ELIZABETH DURNING WALKED IN SHADE ON THE EAST side of Main Street. There was cold early-morning sunlight on the west side where Marshal Fogarty stood at his office window looking out and holding a mug of morning java.

When she entered the cafe, he put the coffee aside and left the jailhouse by the rear door and walked briskly up the back alley as far as the hotel. The town was only beginning to make its customary sounds as he

43

went along the gloomy corridor to Elizabeth Durning's room. He did not encounter anyone, and by a simple method of using a key that would open almost any simple kitchen-door-type lock, got inside.

He could see sunshine far out upon the open range country, but its brilliance did nothing to improve visibility in the hotel room as Fogarty began his search.

Elizabeth Duming was a tidy individual. She had made her bed before going down to the cafe for breakfast. She had also put other things in order, and her quarters were faintly fragrant of a scent Marshal Fogarty associated with the fragrance of that big old bush on the west side of the porch. He tried to remember the name of the fragrance as he searched. He might have remembered it if he hadn't found a Lightning Colt tucked far over near the middle of the bed beneath the thin, pulpy mattress.

His search just about ended there. It might as well have, because he found nothing else of immediate interest, nor did he want to linger any longer than he had to.

Fogarty departed by the door at the rear of the old building, crossed over to the same alley he'd used to get there, and hiked back down to the jailhouse. The only encounter he had in the early-morning chill of breakfast time was with a bony-tailed, slab-sided tan dog who was rummaging among trash bins and fled at the sight of the two-legged animal.

The office stove had just about lost its fire by the time he got back. He put the Lightning Colt on his desk, dropped his hat over it, and was leaning to stir for embers before feeding in some kindling when a visitor walked in from out front. Fogarty did not look around until he had shavings smoking and was placing sticks of

44

fat wood atop them. Then all he said was, "Have a seat, I'll be with you in a minute."

When the first puff of fire emerged, Fogarty straightened up, closed the iron door, made certain his coffeepot was directly over the small stove's solitary burner, and turned.

The cornflower-blue eyes were on him with a faintly amused expression. She evidently thought he would be surprised when he faced around, and she was correct. His eyes widened, clung to her face briefly, then moved to the old hat on the desk. She had the advantage as he went to his desk and sat down, but he got it back when he said, "I thought you were goin' south the day after the Donner shooting."

"I was," she told him, "but first I overslept, then I just plain missed the stage."

He could believe she would oversleep. Anyone who could sleep through the racket he'd made knocking on her door at the hotel was an accomplished sleeper. What he did not believe was that she had accidentally missed those stages, so he said, "I'm glad you're still here, Miss Durning. Enough time's passed for you to recover from what you went through at the bank. I'm hoping you've been able to remember something helpful about that day."

She was clutching a large handbag in her lap and looked down at it when she spoke. "Not about the shooting, Marshal. It happened the way I told you that day. I didn't see anyone but Mr. Donner." Her eyes swept up to his face and remained there. She abruptly changed the subject while holding his gaze. "I came over here to ask a favor of you. When I leave here I'd like to do so by the back door. I'll go down to the livery barn, hire a top buggy, and drive southwest from town to a little creek I found when I drove out of town yesterday. It's almost completely hidden by willows on both banks. There's a dilapidated log shack on the far side of the creek about a quarter mile."

Fogarty was nodding before she finished. "I know the place. Pretty hard to see the shack for the willows."

"I want you to ride out there, but not directly. Ride upcountry until you're out of sight of town, then turn due south on the far side of the creek where no one can see you. I'll be waiting at the log shack."

Marshal Fogarty considered her lovely features—her softly rounded square-set jaw and determined mouth. He smiled at her. "That sounds like an ambush, don't it?" he said, and although she smiled, too, the expression had very little warmth to it.

"It's not an ambush, Marshal. It might be just the opposite. It might be your best chance not to be shot at."

"I see. You wouldn't care to explain a little more, would you?"

She arose, looking past the marshal at the only door in the rear of the room. "I can't. Not now. Not in town. Will you meet me out there?"

As Joe Fogarty rose, his grin was genuine. "Miss Durning, you understand Spanish?"

"A little. Why?"

"Well, you could ask me to meet you at the gates to *el tierra inferno* and I'd do it."

She glanced at him, smiled a little uncertainly, and went to the storeroom door to wait until he opened it for her. He took her through to the back alley, then stood in shadowy gloom watching her walking southward toward the lower end of town where Reg Lee had his barn.

He returned to the office, got a cup of coffee, and

46

stood without raising it for a long time. It *did* sound like an ambush.

He sipped the coffee, removed his hat to pick up the six-gun beneath it, put the cup aside, and sat down to examine the weapon. It was loaded, and it was a fairly new gun. If it had been fired, he found no sign of it.

What furrowed his brow was that while Jack Carpenter had said the woman's weapon had been a nickel-plated Lightning Colt, and Fogarty had found this weapon in her room, it was not plated at all. It was blued.

He put the gun in a drawer, locked the jailhouse from the inside by the simple expedient of an oak *tranca,* got a booted saddle gun, and left by the back alley. On his way southward he met no one, not even any dogs, and when he arrived at the livery barn there was no sign of Reg Lee, but Reg's new hired hostler, Charley Wright, met Fogarty with a little smile and led the way to a shady stall, where the lawman's horse was rigged out and waiting.

Fogarty eyed the horse and turned. Charley Wright was smiling at him. But he said nothing as he opened the door and led the horse out, handed Marshal Fogarty the reins, and walked away.

The marshal took his time about snugging up the cinch and bridling. He draped the halter and shank over the stall door and led his horse out back where the morning sun still had not reached.

He did as the handsome woman had suggested: He left town on a northward course, but began slanting a little westerly as he rode along.

It was a magnificent day. Behind him, lazy drifts of smoke rose over town where breakfast fires had been burning and now seemed to have been damped down or allowed to die.

47

The land was empty except for a bitch-coyote he startled up out of a slight swale. She did her best to race away, but she was heavy; her time was near.

He watched her disappear through tall grass, then he faced in a different direction. He was in no hurry. He had decided to do what was prudent, so he obeyed the woman's suggestion of riding north and a little westerly, but he did not turn south when he finally reached the creek. He crossed it and continued westward until he was on the grazing ground of a man named Amos Bartlett, one of the largest cattlemen in terms of land and livestock in the territory.

He did, eventually, turn southward, but by that time he could no longer see much of the willow creek. He continued southward until the sun had passed overhead, then changed to an easterly course and rode for quite a while before reaching the creek. There he turned northward, masked by willow shade and slanting sun rays until he had the old log house in sight.

He left the horse more than a half mile southward concealed among creek willows and walked along the spongy shoreline where ripgut and weeds reached above his knees, carrying the saddle gun in the bend of one arm.

He saw the top buggy. It had been parked behind the old trapper's shack. The horse was dozing in semishade and did not raise its head even when Fogarty was close enough to hit the house with a rock, if he'd cared to.

He remained concealed among the willows for a while, looking for signs of more than one person being out here. He heard nothing, saw nothing, and sensed nothing. If there was danger, he could not detect it, so he finally did pitch a worn-smooth stone from the creek. It rattled down the dangerously swaybacked roof of the log house and landed in the grass. Nothing happened for a long while.

He was beginning to wonder where she was when he saw her standing back from the doorless opening inside the house. She was standing back there looking out. She had both hands clasped over her stomach in a stance that told Fogarty she was tense.

He rose to call and be ready to move swiftly as he did so. He called her name and was sidestepping before he had finished.

No flurry of bullets came his way. There was no sound at all, not even from the shack, but Elizabeth Durning was now standing squarely in the doorless opening frowning in the direction of the creek. She had one hand on the jamb, the other hand behind her.

Fogarty moved into sight. She saw him and spoke. "It took you nearly all day, Marshal."

He looked around, still uncertain. "Who is with you, ma'am?"

She straightened up, staring at him. "No one is with me. I'm alone."

Fogarty remained among the shadowy willows. "In that case, you walk over here where I am, an' if there's someone back there in the house they'll have to shoot you to hit me."

She stepped forth and approached him looking angry. When she stopped, she said, "There is no one in the house. I told you—I am alone."

Fogarty jutted his chin. "What's in the hand you're holding behind you?"

She brought the hand into plain view. She was holding a nickel-plated Lighning Colt in it. As he watched, she eased aside her riding jacket and pushed the weapon into a holster that was against her left side, lower than the armpit but higher than her waist.

She did not explain why she had been holding the weapon behind her back. She spoke briskly while looking Joe Fogarty squarely in the eye. "It is not an ambush. I told you—"

"Lady, I sort of believe you, but I didn't come down in the last rain and I never saw a livery-barn hostler who could read minds before." He paused to smile thinly at her. "But you got my curiosity up, so, against anyone's better judgment, here I am. "

She ignored the smile. "Charley said you'd be suspicious if your horse was already saddled and waiting. Marshal, I wanted you out here as soon as you could get here."

"An' I wasted darned near the whole day, didn't I? Who is Charley?"

She did not respond until she had palmed a small badge to show him. "He is a deputy U.S. marshal out of Denver."

"That's not a federal badge, Miss Durning."

She was pocketing it as she replied, "Pinkerton Agency."

Fogarty eased his saddle gun to the ground to lean on as he regarded her. "You're full of surprises, lady. You work for the Pinkertons, and Charley Wright is a federal marshal . . . Why?"

She moved into better shade before speaking again. "Maybe we should sit down, Marshal. It's not a long story, but it is a little complicated."

He waited until she was seated, then sank to one knee still leaning on the Winchester. She was going to speak when he cut in to ask a question. "Whose gun was that under your mattress?"

It was her turn to look surprised. "You have it?"

50

"Yes'm. In a drawer at the jailhouse. Did you put it under there?"

"Yes."

"Where did you get it?"

"Out of Mr. Donner's desk drawer. Marshal . . . after he was shot I went back there to search his desk. That gun was in a drawer. I took it and was about to finish searching, when you started yelling from the roadway. I didn't answer for as long as it took me to make a very fast search of his top drawer. You didn't give me any more time than that."

Fogarty looked over toward the house, then back to her face. "What did you find?"

"I just told you. Nothing."

"Why did you take the gun?"

Elizabeth burning raised the back of one hand to brush aside a coil of curly hair. "Because I wasn't sure that when you called it might not be somebody else— whoever shot Mr. Donner. I didn't want to walk out of the bank without at least a chance to stay alive."

Fogarty looked around again, shifted position, got comfortable on the ground, flagged away some mosquitoes with his hat, held the Winchester across his lap, and said, "I get the feelin' we're talkin' around in circles, and the day's wearing along. We're not goin' to get back until after sundown as it is. Miss Durning, I did you a favor, now you do me one: Start at the beginning."

She shifted position slightly, asked where his horse was, and after he had told her she made a statement that he would remember. She said, "Whenever a lot of money is involved, Marshal, life begins to become difficult and keeps right on being that way."

He rummaged for his tobacco sack and papers, telling

51

himself as he worked up a smoke that life not only does get difficult, it also seems to load up on contradictions. He lit up, trickled smoke, and gazed at her.

He had encountered Pinkerton detectives before, and every time they had worn pants. She was, in Joe Fogarty's opinion, the epitome of contradiction. She was as handsome a woman as he had ever seen—and she not only had a badge in her pocket, she also carried a six-gun next to her ribs.

DOUBTS AND QUESTIONS

SHE HAD A CRISP WAY OF SPEAKING. THE LONGER HE sat listening to her, the more he began to suspect that Elizabeth Durning was a serious individual, and that seemed unfortunate to Joe Fogarty: Anyone that pretty should be less businesslike and smile oftener.

"There was supposed to be a packet of money in Mr. Donner's desk. You prevented me from making a thorough search for it."

Fogarty leaned to stub out his smoke as he said, "There was no money in his desk. I went through every drawer. There was a lot of bank papers, some letters, several notes, but no money."

"Then it is probably in the vault," she said, "but it was supposed to be somewhere in the desk." Elizabeth Durning checked herself, considered the bronzed, lanky man sitting in front of her, then said, "Counterfeit money, Marshal."

Fogarty flapped his hat at mosquitoes and waited for her to continue. It was a short wait.

"Denver was being flooded with counterfeit money, Marshal. The federal authorities finally located the

52

building where it was being made down near Colorado Springs. But they could not find the men who had been making the money. They got several descriptions of them and turned that information over to Charley, while they tried to round up as much of the money as they could before it caused a financial panic.

"A group of merchants who stood to lose thousands were not satisfied with the federal marshal's progress, so they went to the Pinkerton Agency. They were a lot less concerned about the flood of counterfeit greenbacks than they were with having the counterfeiters caught. Their complaint was that as long as the U.S. marshal's office was spending all its time trying to gather up the money, the men who had made it were loose and probably setting up their printing presses somewhere else."

She stopped speaking to cock her head in a listening position for a moment, then, because she evidently had only imagined she'd heard something, she was prepared to continue speaking when Marshal Fogarty said, "How did you find out who they were?"

"By doing what the deputy marshals hadn't done very thoroughly. I talked to thirty-five storekeepers who'd taken in the counterfeit notes. Fifteen of them described the same two men. The others gave a variety of descriptions or hadn't actually seen anyone paying for items in their stores.

"But those fifteen descriptions were of one rather dark man, not overly tall, who dressed well and had a cold, almost truculent personality."

Fogarty nodded his head. "Macy."

"Yes. That's not his name, but as far as we're concerned, right now it will do."

"Let me guess, ma'am. The other one's name is William Booker."

She nodded curtly. "Yes. His real name is William Brennan."

"How did you figure out who they were?"

"The agency keeps excellent records. They had both men listed as counterfeiters, including backgrounds and descriptions."

"You told the U.S. marshal in Denver?"

She smiled a little. "No. I asked for a deputy to be assigned to my investigation. When I was ready to leave Denver on their trail, I told him. I also suggested that he search among the stage companies for passengers with those descriptions. What he came up with was better than I could have hoped for. They had not left Denver, and when they finally did show up to buy passage southward, Charley was told. He had a rider's outfit. I didn't need a disguise. I'd never seen either Booker or Macy, and they'd never seen me. We bought passage on the same coach, and except for the descriptions I had, I'd never have thought the pair of traveling salesmen who were on the coach with us were Macy and Booker. They looked and acted exactly like drummers. They even talked like them."

Fogarty held up a hand. "How did you know Peter Donner had some of that counterfeit money?"

"Because he'd evidently discovered it among bills the bank had taken in. He sent two bills to the marshal's office in Denver. They told Charley."

Fogarty looked steadily at the handsome woman. "Counterfeit greenbacks are pretty common. I expect we all receive them an' pass them along from time to time. An' I can believe Pete Donner would be able to detect homemade money. But . . . why would Macy and Booker head down here to Sheridan? Is this where they figured to set up their homemade-money business

54

again? What's really got me stumped is why they'd shoot Pete Donner."

The handsome woman showed a very sweet smile when she replied. "That is why I wanted to meet you out here today, Marshal. I don't have the answers. All I know is that Sheridan is where they came, have not yet left, and the man who warned the authorities in Denver that some of that counterfeit money was down here got shot the day after Charley and I arrived. We came on the same coach Macy and Booker arrived in."

Fogarty slowly and silently rolled a smoke, lit it, and looked steadily at Elizabeth Durning. "I don't think that's all of it, Miss Durning. You said you wanted to search Donner's desk. Well, now, you'd have been lookin' for the rest of that money, an' you said it was supposed to be in his desk. How did you know that?"

The sweet smile remained in place. "Because in the letter Mr. Donner wrote to Denver, he said he would have the money in his desk to hand over to anyone the U.S. marshal sent down here. He was very insistent in the letter. I have a copy of it Charley made before we left Denver. Now, Marshal, you've been interested in the shooting. How could someone have shot Mr. Donner when I was in the outer section of the bank with him in my sight, and not be visible to me?"

Fogarty killed his smoke against the spongy earth. "I don't know. But I'm goin' to find out." He rose and brushed himself off; dusk was approaching. "Is that why Booker and Macy are hangin' around town, because they want those counterfeit notes?"

Elizabeth Durning also rose. "Marshal, those men probably have them."

Fogarty's eyes widened on her.

"I didn't find the notes. You didn't find any money in

his desk. They were supposed to be there. Mr. Donner said in his letter that they would be and they weren't." Her very blue eyes remained on his face. "Did you have a man stay inside the bank the night after the shooting? No. It's possible that Booker and Macy either were already inside or got inside that night, got the money, and—"

"Wait a minute. You didn't find any money in the desk."

"I told you—I didn't have time to make a thorough search."

"Well, ma'am, I had the time an' I looked in every drawer, an' there was no money."

She smiled very sweetly again. "Did you? The day of the shooting?"

He looked around, lifted his hat, and replaced it.

Her smile deepened. "I thought not. You searched the day after the shooting."

Fogarty frowned. He'd known none of this the day of the shooting or the day following. Until he'd met her out here, he'd had no idea of any of this. Donner's shooting had seemed to him to be an attempted assassination. It was not hard to accept something like that, because Pete Donner was an unpopular man in town and beyond it, out over the open range. Vengeful human beings were a penny a dozen.

Elizabeth Durning scanned the smoky heavens. "We'd better go back," she said, and added one more word. "Separately."

Fogarty watched her walk toward the dilapidated log structure and disappear behind it. He turned southward, remaining among the willows even though he really did not believe anyone had seen them together out here or had followed him from town.

He cinched the horse, set the bridle, looped the hobbles through the rear rigging rings behind the cantle and down each side, then stood listening to the top buggy rattle across the creek heading west.

There was no particular need for haste, so he remained behind for almost a full hour before mounting and reining in the wake of the rig. He had lots to speculate about. Also, there were aspects of what she had told him that posed questions rather than offered answers.

He did not doubt her, but he made up his mind long before sighting Sheridan's lighted windows that he was going to round up those two drummers, take them to the jailhouse, and have a long talk with them. If she'd told the truth, they could verify it.

When he led his horse in out of the darkness, Charley Wright was waiting in the runway's flickering lamplight. He smiled straight into Fogarty's eyes and, without a word passing between them, led the horse away.

Over at the cafe, the proprietor had three diners; it was late for most of his customers. He was making trips back and forth between his curtained-off area and the counter, carrying dishes and cups away. He glanced up at Marshal Fogarty without acknowledging that they knew one another and continued with his work until Fogarty told him he wanted supper.

The other diners left. The cafeman refilled Fogarty's cup and put aside the pot as he said, "Never fails; when the cat is away, the mice play."

Fogarty raised his head, chewed tough meat, and waited.

"Someone tried to kill Mr. Donner this evening, about dusk. The way I heard it, they crept up beneath the

57

window, raised it up, and fired at him in the bed."

Fogarty's food lay forgotten in his mouth. He spoke around it. "Kill him?"

The surly cafeman crossed brawny arms over his chest and made a smile that looked like his face was tearing. "Didn't even come close. He was in the outhouse out back. I guess the bunched-up blankets looked like he was in 'em. The story I heard in here, when the place was full this evening, was that whoever he was, he fired off two rounds and liked to tore Miz Pohl's blankets all to hell."

Fogarty pushed the platter away, drained the cup as he was rising, tossed coins atop the counter, and departed. The cafeman threw back his head and laughed.

Dr. Pohl verified what the cafeman had said. He showed Fogarty the room, the window through which the gunman had fired, and the ruined bedding.

Fogarty went to the window to look out. Except for a thick old stand of hedge below the window, the view was unobstructed all the way to the road beyond. As he was turning back, Henry Pohl said dryly that while he believed it was much too late to do much, if Joe was interested there were boot tracks leading from the alley around through his wife's geranium beds to the front window, and back again to the alley.

Fogarty did not look for the tracks. Even if darkness had not pretty well precluded the possibility of his being able to see very much, he had a fair idea of who had tried the bushwhack and why they had done it. He asked about Pete Donner, and Dr. Pohl's eyes twinkled for the first time all day.

"He's been able to look after himself a little since yesterday. No exertion, mind, and back into bed the moment he's told to. We'd had supper, and Pete was out back when the gunman attacked from out front. Pete came back into the house breathing like he'd run a mile. My wife took him in tow and guided him to the bedroom. When they opened the door, she lighted a lamp, saw what someone had done, particularly to a quilt her mother had made for her after we were married, and she was so furious she turned on the nearest object, which was Pete Donner. Later, when I took him to the lean-to room off the kitchen and put him to bed, he said he'd never been talked to like that before in his whole life."

Fogarty smiled in appreciation of Mrs. Pohl's wrath, as he was expected to do, then asked if Donner was able to see a visitor. Evidently he was, because Dr. Pohl turned toward the door of the blown-apart bedroom and led the way to the rear of the house and through the kitchen toward a little doorway in the north wall.

His wife was at the sink when the men passed through. She returned Joe Fogarty's nod with a forced smile and went back to her work.

Swarthy Pete Donner squinted his eyes when Dr. Pohl lighted a small bedside lamp. He put a caustic gaze upon the lawman. Instead of greeting him he said, "Half the town tried to find you this evening, Marshal."

Fogarty accepted the implied rebuke without difficulty. He and the banker had never been more than acquaintances, and they'd exchanged sharp words before, but right now he was not concerned with their mutual dislike. When he spoke, Donner's eyes sprang wide open and Dr. Pohl turned slowly to regard the marshal with a baffled expression.

Fogarty said, "Why didn't you come to me with that homemade money, Pete?"

Donner's reply was delayed. He had to realize from the question that Marshal Fogarty had at least some general knowledge of something Donner had kept in confidence. When he finally answered, his reply was more nearly a question than an answer.

"What do you think would have happened if word spread that counterfeit money was in circulation? Everyone with savings at the bank would have taken their money out."

Fogarty's brows drew together. "In circulation? Here in Sheridan?"

"Well, I don't know, but that money I hid in the desk was counterfeit, and it was deposited by local people."

Fogarty shoved back his hat. The lady detective had said nothing about there being more of that money in town. Fogarty had to balance a judgment; either she had known there was more of it around and had not told him or Pete Donner had been imagining things. He changed the subject. "Who shot you?"

Donner looked Fogarty straight in the eye when he answered. "I don't know. One minute I was sitting at my desk, and the next minute I got shot. That's all I remember."

"Did you see the woman in front of the clerk's cage?"

Donner's gaze did not waver. "A woman? I didn't see any woman. It started out to be a hectic day. First off, the clerk was sick, then I'd been expectin' some federal lawmen to arrive in town, then a dog fight erupted in the space between the bank and McGregor's gun shop. On top of those things I had considerable paperwork to tend to while also minding the clerk's cage."

"There was no one inside the railing? You didn't see anyone maybe over by the vault or the doorway leading out back?"

"Joe, I didn't see anyone. No woman and certainly no one inside the railing."

Fogarty glanced at Henry Pohl, who'd been following this exchange with interest, then looked back toward the bed. He had another question for the banker. "I didn't find any money in your desk. Where was it?"

"You have to remove the top drawer on the left side. There's a special empty place that goes all the way down. It's between the back of the drawer and the back of the desk."

Fogarty reset his hat as he was turning away. He was in the doorway looking back when he said, "Why do you think someone wants you dead enough to bushwhack you twice?"

Donner did not hesitate when he replied this time. He had already reached a conclusion about that. "Because of that damned money. I can't think of any other reason. But how they knew I had it, or that I knew it was counterfeit, I got no idea." He made a parting shot at the marshal. "That's your job. You find the answers."

ONE MYSTERY RESOLVED

THE GUNSMITH AND THE HARNESSMAKER WERE FACING the narrow dogtrot between McGregor's gun works and the bank's north wall when Joe Fogarty arrived at the bank. He stopped when Hugh Pepperdine called his name and beckoned. McGregor said dryly, "Joe, a couple of town mongrels got into a ruckus down there the day Pete got shot. I broke it up with a scantling."

Fogarty nodded. He already knew about the dog fight.

The gunsmith and the harnessmaker exchanged a glance. Hugh nodded, and James McGregor jerked his

61

head for Fogarty to follow him as he stepped down into the perpetually gloomy, long, narrow runway that led from Main Street to the back alley. Pepperdine walked behind the lawman. There was barely more than shoulder room as McGregor halted and faced the bank's north wall. He raised a finger and pointed. He did not say a word and neither did Hugh Pepperdine. They didn't have to.

Someone had left fresh shavings in the dogtrot where they had bored a hole through the bank's wall at about shoulder height. Fogarty removed his hat, leaned to put his eye to the hole, and could see perfectly across the inner working area of the bank to Pete Donner's desk.

He tried looking elsewhere, but while the hole allowed excellent straight-ahead visibility, it was not possible to see to either side very well.

McGregor waited until Joe Fogarty straightened to say, "A man couldn't use a carbine in here. The dogtrot's too narrow, but stick your thumb through that hole, Joe. A man could get a six-gun barrel through real easy with somethin' to spare. What Hugh an' I was discussin' when you came along was that whoever hid in here and made that hole must have spent some time figurin' the exact placement an' angle so that when he fired he'd hit whoever was across the room at Donner's desk. He had to figure real well because most likely he'd never get a second chance if he missed the first time."

Fogarty said nothing. He signaled for Hugh to reverse himself and lead the way back to sunshine. Out there, Fogarty eyed the pair of older men. "You found that hole the day Pete was shot?" he asked McGregor, and got an indignant glare when the gunsmith answered.

"I did no such a thing. I didn't discover it until yesterday afternoon when some confounded drunk from

Rusty's place ducked down in there to pee. I saw him go in there. I've had trouble with people doin' that for years. The place got to smellin' worse'n Jim Young's tanyard. I ran him off; chased him on down through to the alley, and came back up through. That's when I noticed the shavings underfoot, looked up, and there was the hole. I told Hugh. We went lookin' around town for you last night and couldn't find you."

Fogarty's mood lightened. "I'm obliged," he told the gunsmith. "I couldn't figure out how Donner got shot right there at his desk with a woman standin' by the clerk's cage and no one saw the bushwhacker nor the gun."

Hugh Pepperdine was skiving a chew off his cut plug when he spoke. "James'n I talked before you came along." Hugh waited to say more until his cud was securely tongued into place. Then, with his pale, shrewd little eyes fixed on the marshal, he continued speaking. "Joe, you might have gone five years an' never used this dogtrot nor seen that hole. You might never have found it, an' therefore it would have always been a mystery how that bushwhacker shot Mr. Donner. Ten, twenty years from now folks would still be tryin' to figure out how that gunman—"

Fogarty interrupted. "When you said you two 'd been talking before I came along, I knew I wasn't goin' to like what you came up with."

Old Pepperdine spread his hands, palms down, and smiled around his bulging right cheek. "We done you a favor, Joe. We maybe even handed you the key to a bushwhack . . . Do you expect a full quart of malt whiskey would be about the right fee for a couple of gents who've practically solved the Donner shootin' for you?"

Fogarty looked from one of them to the other. Pepperdine, the raffish, shrewd one of the pair, was expectantly smiling. His friend the gunsmith was not smiling at all, but then James McGregor rarely smiled, anyway.

"I expect you want me to go right now, buy the bottle, and bring it back to you," Fogarty said, and was immediately answered by both older men.

"No. Nothin' like that at all. We'll go get the bottle an' tell Rusty you'll pay for it. Your time's valuable, Joe. You got a near murder on your hands. The fact that we've about half solved it for you don't mean you ain't got other loose ends to tie up. All right? We can tell Rusty you'll pay for the bottle?"

Fogarty nodded, turned, and walked down to the bank doorway. He did not look back. If he had, he'd have seen one of McGregor's very rare smiles. Both older men were smiling.

The clerk looked up when Marshal Fogarty walked in. They exchanged a nod as Joe pushed past the little ornamental gate of the railing that separated the inner and outer areas of the bank.

Locating the hole in the north wall did not require a lot of time, but because there were dark knots in the paneling, Fogarty had to stand for a moment looking from one to the other until he found a brown knot with a gun-barrel-size hole in the center of it.

There were a few scattered curls of wood shavings, which was unavoidable even though the whittler had been very careful that most of the whittlings fell into the dogtrot.

Fogarty turned away and saw the clerk watching him. Two women carrying net shopping bags entered, and the clerk sat forward again.

Fogarty approached the desk, stood gazing at it until the female customers had departed, then leaned to work the first drawer free of the desk. The clerk swiveled around to stare. Fogarty had removed each drawer before he could get his hand and arm back through to grope for the opening Donner had mentioned.

When he found it, his arm was not long enough to reach to the bottom, so he pushed the desk over onto its back, lifted out his six-gun, and, using the barrel to knock some wood loose, was able to reach down there.

The clerk's jaw was hanging slack as he watched Marshal Fogarty twist his upper body to extend his groping hand and to eventually pull back clutching a bundle of greenbacks tied together by a piece of ordinary grocer's twine.

Fogarty set the desk back upright, but left the drawers scattered, as he pocketed the packet of money, nodded to the clerk, and left the bank.

Over at his jailhouse office, Fogarty barred the door from the inside, lighted his table lamp, although sunshine was entering from out front, and removed the twine from Pete Donner's little packet.

He held the greenbacks to the lamplight. He tried to smudge them. He snapped the paper between his fingers and finally dropped the bills to the desk and stared at them. They looked genuine to him. He stared a little longer, wondering if maybe Donner was mistaken, if those notes were perfectly genuine, until he remembered that Donner had sent some to Denver and up there they had been pronounced counterfeit.

Donner would have to explain to Fogarty how he could detect counterfeit money from sound money, when to Joe Fogarty the homemade articles looked perfectly genuine.

He put the money in a safe place and walked over to Rusty's saloon. The only other customer at the bar was Silas Browning from over at the stage office. Silas was nursing a jolt glass of sarsaparilla, occasionally sipping from it as though he might have been drinking wine. It put Joe Fogarty's teeth on edge to watch him drink like that.

They exchanged a grunt and a nod before Rusty came along wearing one of his elegant vests, this one with appliqué added to the brocade roses. Fogarty asked for beer, and when Morton went to draw it off, the old man nearby made his little sniffing sound and muttered, "I never trusted a grown man wearin' a necktie or a vest like that."

Fogarty said nothing. Silas was old enough to find very little in this life he either admired or approved of.

When his beer arrived, Fogarty drank half of it, looked at the eye-smarting vest, and sighed. Morton said, "Hugh an' James got a bottle an' said you'd pay for it."

Fogarty counted out the money and placed it beside his beer glass. As the barman reached for the money, he did not come right out and ask what McGregor and Pepperdine had done to earn that bottle; he simply said, "It ain't even Christmas. They must have done you a big favor."

Fogarty finished his beer, looked around, and asked if either of those drummers who'd been in town over the past few days had been in.

Before Rusty could reply, old Silas spoke up. "One of 'em bought a ride south on the evenin' coach."

Fogarty looked around. "The dark one, the feller called Macy?"

"I don't ask names. He's not very dark. Taller'n the other one."

66

Fogarty faced the back bar. That would be William Booker, the more relaxed and congenial of the pair. "How far south is he going, Silas?"

"I got no idea, but he paid for a ride down to some town with a Mex name near the border. I wrote the town down, but, hell, I never could pronounce those names."

Fogarty had one final question. "What time does the evening stage leave tonight?"

Silas was sipping and made no attempt to reply until his little glass was empty. Then he said, "It's supposed to leave right at six o'clock, but with Jack Carpenter toolin' the thing, your guess is as good as mine." Old Browning then launched into a complaint about stage drivers. He was still complaining when Joe Fogarty left the saloon.

Of one thing he was certain: Neither one of those drummers was going to leave Sheridan until he'd talked to them both, and maybe after that they wouldn't be able to leave town.

Someone was in his office across the road. He saw the door ajar and thought he saw movement inside, so he hiked over there.

His visitor was the hostler named Charley Wright. When Fogarty entered, the lean, permanently bronzed face of his visitor brightened slightly. Wright sat down, pushed out his feet, and said, "Well, Miss Durning met me last night for a palaver. I guess you know as much as we know. Maybe more. Anyway, she wants you to wait until the hotel is quiet tonight, then slip up to her room." Charley Wright eyed Joe Fogarty with a perfectly expressionless face. "There's somethin' goin' on between Macy an' Booker. Macy rented a little building over behind the tanyard. He told the feller who owns the tanyard that him and his partner need a place to store

67

some sale items. He told him they figure to set up here in Sheridan and peddle in all directions, using the little building as a sort of storehouse." Wright was studying his scuffed old boots when he said the rest of it. "Miss Durning thinks those big sample cases they lug with them have at least part of their money-printing equipment in them."

Wright shot up to his feet. "I'm goin' to scout it out tonight. I don' think she's right, but I promised I'd look in there, anyway. She'll be expectin' you, Marshal."

As Reg Lee's hired man reached the roadway door, Joe Fogarty asked him a question. "Did you ever work with a lady Pinkerton before?"

The answer was crisp. "No, sir, I never did. An' I'm not excited about doin' it this time. But a man's got to give the devil his due: She can figure things."

After Wright's departure, Fogarty had a thoughtful smoke before going up to the corralyard to look for Silas Browning. He found the gnomelike manager beneath a battered, old, faded stagecoach with another man. They were examining an axle that had struck something, probably a boulder, with sufficient force to knock the U-bolt blocks askew. The coached had limped into town with both rear wheels making separate tracks from the front wheels.

Silas saw the marshal's leg, climbed out, stood up, and beat dirt off his backside. Fogarty took him slightly apart from the man he'd been beneath the coach with and said, "Don't let that peddler leave town tonight, Silas. If the other one shows up, don't sell him a seat, either."

Browning looked up crankily and sniffed. "Just like that I'm supposed to refuse to—"

"Just like that."

"Marshal, if you want them boys, why don't you go find them, arrest them, and take them back to the jailhouse with you? Me, I run a stage line. I don't ask no questions. I just hold out my hand an' if folks drop enough silver into it to pay for wherever they want to go, why, that's what I'm in business for."

Fogarty was accustomed to the old man's waspishness and ignored it now as he'd done other times. "One of them is supposed to show up tonight. I just want your cooperation in case I can't find them before nightfall."

"Find them? You must sleep a lot in your jailhouse, Marshal. The both of 'em walked past here a half hour back headin' for the cafe. Not alone. There was a bearded feller with them who was wearin' one of them checkered or plaid shirts, whatever you want to call 'em. He looked to me like a freighter. He was wearing walkin' boots for one thing, and had a dust bandanna around his neck. I'm not a wagerin' man. In my church gamblin' is a real bad sin. But if I was a wagerin' man, I'd give you thirty-to-one odds that feller is a freighter, not just someone who looks like one."

Fogarty headed for the cafe. According to the cafeman, he was ten minutes too late. The drummers and their companion with all the face feathers had been talking about one of them leaving town for a few days. The cafeman knew no more. There had been a half-dozen hungry customers at his counter at the time the drummers were in there. He had no idea where they had gone.

Fogarty was walking up to the hotel when Henry Pohl hailed him from the porch and beckoned. When they met, the doctor said, "Pete wants to see you."

Fogarty was agreeable. He wanted to find out how

69

money that looked like the genuine article could be detected as being counterfeit.

The day was ending. Not rapidly, but slowly, and actual visibility would not be impaired for several hours after sunset, because spring was already yielding to summer.

THAT WOMAN AGAIN

BEFORE THEY REACHED THE LEAN-TO BEDROOM OFF the kitchen, Dr. Pohl stopped and said, "He's afraid. I'm not sure that I blame him."

Fogarty understood. "There aren't any windows in the lean-to."

"But he uses the outhouse."

Fogarty eyed Henry Pohl. "If he's well enough, I can take him to the jailhouse and lock him in a cell. He'll be safe down there."

The doctor shrugged. "You can suggest it," he said, and would have moved along, but Fogarty caught him by the arm. "What does he want to see me about?"

"About getting shot at again. That was a close call."

Donner looked sallow rather than pale. He was obviously making a steady but slow recovery. His voice, eyes, and evidently his mind as well were not the least inhibited. When Henry Pohl left Joe Fogarty in the room with Donner and closed the door so they would have privacy, Donner said, "It's been several days, Joe. Surely by now you've come up with something."

Fogarty stood relaxed and hipshot, thumbs hooked in his shell belt, gazing at the man in the narrow little bed. What he had "come up with" he had no intention of sharing with Pete Donner.

70

"Tell me how you could tell that money was counterfeit, Pete. I got it over at the jailhouse. It looks like sound money to me."

Donner's interest was not in the money, it was in staying alive. He ignored the question to say, "He's still out there, isn't he? Henry said there was boot tracks. Did you look at them?"

"No. It was too dark when I got up here and since then I've been too busy."

Donner's color heightened. His dark brown eyes were riveted on Marshal Fogarty. "Too busy? What you got to be too busy about except what happened to me?"

Fogarty met the menacing stare without difficulty and repeated his earlier query. "How could you tell that it was homemade money?"

"Did you compare it? Did you put a genuine greenback directly above one of those notes and compare them? No, of course you didn't. You're too busy. Go back and make a comparison. You'll see that one note is not genuine. And after you've done that, remember that I'm still lyin' up here like a hen on a nest for some weasel with a six-gun to shoot at."

"What will I see by comparing notes?"

"That the numbers were not printed. They were put on the money by hand. Look close. You'll see other places where a damned fine calligrapher used a pen, where on good money everything has been printed."

Fogarty nodded. He had his answer about the money. He now made a suggestion that made more color pump into the banker's swarthy face. "Pete, there's only one place I know of in town where you'll be plumb safe. At the jailhouse. Down in the cell room. Even if I'm not in the office, no one could get at you down in there unless they used dynamite. That steel-strapped oak door

71

leading from my office down into the cell room can't be prized open, or shot open; even that big brass padlock can't be crowbarred open."

Donner glared. "Before I'd let you lock me in one of those little cages I'd hire some bodyguards."

Joe Fogarty gazed a long moment at the banker, then walked out, closed the door after himself, and was already as far as the front parlor before Henry caught up with him. Pohl did not speak, but he raised his brows in a silent query. Fogarty shook his head. "He wants to stay here an' hire a couple of bodyguards."

The doctor's brows dropped. "Marshal, he's on the mend. There's nothing more I can do except look in on him from time to time, make sure an infection doesn't take hold. Otherwise, it is a matter of waiting. Maybe a month, maybe less. He has an iron constitution. Otherwise he'd already be dead." Henry Pohl paused, clearly picking the words he had yet to say with great care. "You haven't found the man who tried to kill him?"

"No. But I will."

"Well. Yes, I believe you will, but in the meantime I have to think of my wife's safety and my own. Marshal, I'm really sorry, but after what happened here, Mr. Donner can't stay here any longer."

Fogarty accepted that because he'd had a hunch when Henry paused before finishing what he had to say, that the attempted murder had shaken both Henry and his wife. He told the doctor more about his offer to house Donner at the jailhouse and how indignantly Pete had reacted.

Henry's response was, "I hope you understand, Joe, but even if I agreed to keep him, hiring bodyguards could very well turn our place into a shooting gallery. If he won't let you put him in a safe place . . ."

72

Fogarty raised his eyes to the gently swinging pendulum of a large wall clock. He said, "Talk to him. I've got something else to look into. Good night, Henry."

Dr. Pohl remained in place until after the roadside door had closed behind Marshal Fogarty, then went in search of his wife.

Fogarty looked southward where someone had lighted the pair of brass carriage lamps on either side of the corralyard gate. That had been old Silas Browning's signal for years that a stage was being readied for departure inside the yard.

He had probably spent too much time with Pete Donner. He turned northward toward the hotel, reached the dilapidated porch, and had a hand out to open the door when a quiet voice spoke from the dark shadows along the west side of the porch where that overpoweringly fragrant lilac bush grew.

"It's a trap, Marshal."

He turned slowly, could not see her until she moved from beyond the porch, came around the big old bush, and spoke again. "Booker's not going to leave town."

When she turned, he followed. They halted beyond the lilac bush and she turned to face him. In the murky dusk she looked ten years younger, and perhaps except for the slight bulge under her light coat on the left side, he would have thought of her as a girl.

She did not raise her voice to him. "They paid for passage on the evening stage. They also mentioned around town that one of them would be leaving town for a few days. Right now they have a man in the back alley where he can see into the yard so that when you walk in to stop Booker from leaving Sheridan, they will know that you are a danger to them. If you don't show up in the yard, they'll be satisfied that you haven't become suspicious."

Fogarty shoved back his hat, looked around, then back. "How do you know this?"

"Very simply. My room is next to Macy's room. That's where they meet. I did a little work on my side of the wall so that I could hear what was said."

Joe blew out a ragged breath and wagged his head at her.

She smiled at him. "We belong to different areas of the same kind of work. I'd never ride down horse thieves. I'd never even attempt to catch rustlers. I certainly wouldn't barge into a saloon on Saturday night and arrest drunken cowboys."

He turned to gaze in the direction of the west-side alley. She said, "Don't do it, Marshal. I suppose you could do it, whether he's armed or not, but if you do, and if he doesn't return to tell them you didn't come to the corralyard, it will tell them the same thing, won't it? That you do indeed know something about them."

Fogarty turned back. She was no longer smiling. She seemed to be waiting for him to say something. He obliged her. "They're pretty skittish, aren't they?"

"Yes. If they weren't, I suppose that by now they would be in prison. I told you out at the willow creek they're experienced outlaws. Men like that develop a sixth sense. That's how they escaped being caught in Colorado Springs and Denver. They are as wary as wolves."

He felt for his makings, decided against a smoke, and smiled woodenly. "All right. The main thing is that they don't leave town."

"They would have if you'd appeared in the corralyard, Marshal. By morning they would be long

74

gone, and neither Charley and I have been on this trail for as long as we have so that some well-meaning, very direct local town marshal can ruin it for us."

Joe Fogarty regarded her stonily for a moment before saying, "Whatever Charley finds in that shack they rented from Jim Young, I'd like to know about."

"You will," she assured him, and waited, but he had no more questions. He brushed the brim of his hat to her, turned, and went back over to the Main Street plank walk and walked southward.

While they had been talking, old Silas had wearied of waiting for the drummer who had paid for passage and not shown up. He had wigwagged with an upraised arm for his driver to head out.

The coach was at the lower end of town. Fogarty could barely make out its outline, but he could smell roiled roadway dust, and by the time he got over to Morton's saloon, the coach was no longer in sight.

The saloon had its usual midweek customers, nearly all townsmen. There was very little noise. Hank Dennis was at the bar beside Hugh Pepperdine. The town blacksmith and wheelwright was nursing a glass of watered whiskey and carrying on a desultory conversation with James McGregor.

There were a couple of card games in session. At one table they were playing Pedro. At the other table it was straight draw poker.

Rusty had changed vests since morning. The one he was now wearing showed brocade vines of some kind, perhaps grape vines, artistically and elegantly intertwining. When he brought Fogarty a bottle and a jolt glass, his face was sweatshiny and he was smiling. "Anyone take a potshot at Pete today?"

Fogarty did not smile as he reached for the bottle to

tip it above the shot glass. "No," he replied flatly. "No one took a potshot at Pete today."

Rusty's smile crumpled. He went briskly up to the bar, convinced that this was a good night to leave Marshal Fogarty strictly alone.

He was right, but it had nothing to do with Pete Donner. At least his sour mood was not directly attributable to Pete Donner. That damned lady detective pussyfooted around doing things men would think twice about, like maybe making a hole in a wall so she could eavesdrop on what was being said in a hotel room.

And she had it all figured out about that friend of Macy's and Booker's who was down the alley spying on the corralyard.

Fogarty downed his jolt and refilled the little glass.

Who in hell was he? Old Silas had said he was a freighter. What would Macy and Booker have to do with a freighter?

Fogarty's hand went to the little glass and remained there as he stared at himself in the back-bar mirror. A freighter could move objects stage companies would not haul. Heavy objects. Maybe as heavy and bulky as printing presses.

He downed the whiskey, shoved the glass and bottle away, put some coins beside them, and left the saloon. Pepperdine and McGregor watched him depart. Behind them, across the bar, Rusty leaned and said, "He's in a bad mood tonight."

Fogarty went over to his office, lighted the lamp, went out back to unbar the alley entrance, and on his way back left the storeroom door open, too.

He stirred up a fire beneath his coffeepot, sat down, and waited. When Charley Wright arrived, he should have something worthwhile to say. Maybe.

But Fogarty's visitor was not Charley Wright, and he entered from the roadway, not the alley. He was wearing a greatly oversized hat for his size, and his faded eyes puckered nearly closed when the glow of the office light hit him in the face. He felt for the chair that had been there for ten years, eased down, looked out from beneath the brim of his grotesque hat, and said, "Well, I figure you must have nailed him since he never showed up to go south on the stage." Old Silas sniffed. "He may not have seen the sign on the front gate. No refunds. We hold a coach for ten minutes. If they don't show up by then, the rig leaves without 'em and the company don't make no refunds."

Fogarty eyed Silas Browning impassively. It was hard to like Silas. He could have been born cranky. If so, that condition had steadily improved over more than a half century until it could be said of Silas Browning that through dedicated nurturing he had achieved the epitome of disagreeableness.

He peeked from beneath the wide hat brim. "Well?"

Fogarty rocked forward to lean on his desk. "Well, what? He didn't show up. You've had it happen before, Silas."

"Yes, I have. But not when a lawman was after someone. Now, you got him in one of your cells?"

Fogarty began methodically to build a smoke. The old man watched until Fogarty was preparing to fire up, then he made his sniffing sound and said, "Cigareets. Men don't smoke cigareets, women do. I was in the war down in Messico. Pretty young then, an' comin' from a decent, upright Baptist family, I seen the world for the first time. Women down there rolled cigareets. Right out in plain sight, mind you. Stood there makin' eyes at you an' rollin' a cigareet."

77

Fogarty let his match die and placed the quirley in a smashed-flat tomato can he used for an ashtray: "What did the men smoke?"

"They smoked cigareets, too, but only the poor folks. Otherwise they smoked stogies. When we was in bivouac before a battle, a man could smell their cigars in the darkness."

"Bad smell, Silas?"

"Well, no. I never smoked. It's against my religion. But that stogie smoke was pleasant to smell. Not cigareets; they got no fragrance, just a stink. But cigars . . ." Silas squinted. "You got him in one of your cells, Marshal?"

Fogarty was reaching for the quirley when he replied. "No. Not yet."

"What is he wanted for?"

"I just wanted to talk to him, is all." Joe lit up, exhaled smoke from the side of his mouth, and old Silas struggled up to his feet.

"No refunds. You tell him that. He held up the southbound for ten minutes. Company rule, Marshal. No refunds."

Fogarty watched Silas close the door after himself, then went to see if the coffee was hot. It was. He filled a dented tin cup, and took it back to the desk with him, and sat down in comfort to wait.

PACKING UP LOOSE ENDS

FOGARTY DUG OUT THE MONEY HE'D TAKEN FROM that hiding place in Donner's desk, selected a note, dug out one of equal denomination from his pocket, pulled the lamp close, and placed the sound greenback above the counterfeit one.

78

He sat a long time comparing them, leaned back to rub his eyes, and muttered under his breath to the effect that only Pete Donner would take the time to sit down and compare greenbacks.

But Donner was right, the lower note had numbers painstakingly drawn by hand, something that would not be noticed by most people. Fogarty thought the forgeries were very good. He also thought that anyone as talented as the man who did the hand lettering on the counterfeit bills would certainly be able to make a very good living as an engraver or maybe working on lithographs. Maybe even touching up pictures.

He made several comparisons. Eventually he put the counterfeit bills away and got more coffee. Outside, Sheridan was settling in for the night. He took the coffee with him to the roadway door, where he leaned in overhang darkness taking the pulse of his town.

Waiting was part of any lawman's job. Sometimes a very big part of it. But that did not make it popular, particularly with men like Joe Fogarty.

When he had drained the cup, he turned back into the office and kicked the door closed.

Charley Wright was sitting in the same chair Silas Browning had vacated earlier. He grinned at Fogarty's startled look. "Nice night, Marshal. Not too hot an' not too cold. Is there any more coffee in that pot?"

Fogarty went around to his desk chair as he waved toward the stove. "Help yourself."

"Didn't mean to come up on you like that, Marshal."

"The hell you didn't."

Charley Wright laughed as he returned to the chair with a cup of coffee. "I saw Miss Durning. She told me she waylaid you on your way up to roust Macy and Booker at the hotel." The lean, perpetually bronzed man sipped coffee for a moment before continuing to speak. "She's smart as a whip."

Fogarty leaned on the desk. "Uh-huh. Charley, when I first started out, an old man told me something I've never forgot. In this life, with all its troubles and tribulations, there are four things a man don't need: a biting dog, a kicking mule, a bucking saddlehorse, an' a smart woman."

The deputy federal marshal sat a moment gazing into his half-empty cup before speaking. "Well, I had a close call at that shed behind the tanyard. I was ready to get inside when Booker showed up with a husky, bearded man. They went inside and didn't leave for more than an hour. I waited another hour to be as positive as I could be that they weren't comin' back."

Fogarty leaned on his elbows. "But you got inside."

"Yeah. Those big sample cases Booker and Macy brought with them are in there. I opened them. One had samples of women's shoes and whatnot. The other one had five Lightning Colt pistols and some catalogs with drawings of smithy supplies and wagon parts."

"That's all?"

Wright inclined his head. "That's all that was in the sample cases. There were a pair of little steel-bound boxes like stage companies use to transport bullion in."

"What was in them?"

Wright returned for more coffee and replied while at the stove. "I don't know. They are heavier'n hell." He faced around. "The only way I could have opened those boxes was to blow off the padlocks."

Fogarty leaned back with nothing to say until the deputy had returned to his chair. "What did Miss Durning say about that?"

"I haven't seen her since before I went up there."

Wright's eyes came up. "Did you meet her at her room tonight?"

"No. Didn't see any reason to after she ambushed me on the hotel porch."

Charley Wright drank his coffee, then put the cup on the edge of Fogarty's desk. Joe Fogarty hid a yawn behind an upraised hand. He'd waited half the damned night for nothing. All those sample cases proved was what he already knew: Booker and Macy had rented a shed from Jim Young. He eyed the lean, darkly tanned man. His immediate reaction to his association with the deputy U.S. marshal and the Pinkerton lady was to let them go their own way while he went up to Jim Young's shed with a crowbar and broke open those bullion boxes.

The federal officer may have surmised something about this reaction on the town marshal's part because he said, "Let it be for tonight. They're not goin' anywhere, an' we got to have better evidence than what we got." Having gotten that off his chest, he scowled faintly and mentioned something else. "Marshal, two things that are hangin' and rattlin' for me. The first one is, how did they know Donner had some of their fake money? The second thing is, how did they know Donner knew it was counterfeit?"

Fogarty hid another yawn before speaking. "All I can tell you right now is that Pete Donner, for some damned reason, takes random greenbacks and examines them. He didn't say he always does this and I didn't ask if he does, but I know Pete Donner. He wouldn't trust his own mother. How he happened to come on to those particular greenbacks I got no idea. But that he sits back there at his desk like a damned spider doin' things like comparing greenbacks don't surprise me one bit."

Wright eyed Fogarty with a shrewd look. That the town marshal was not fond of the town banker had just been made clear. But what the marshal had just said supplied an answer to only one of Wright's questions. The least critical one. "All right. They tried to kill him because they knew he had discovered some of their homemade money. Now tell me how in hell they knew that. He didn't tell you. It seems to me he didn't tell anyone. He sent some notes to Denver to be examined. Donner and the authorities in Denver knew. How the hell did Macy and Booker find out Donner knew about their counterfeit money when he didn't let anyone down here know?"

Fogarty eyed the other man a trifle pensively. "He might have told someone else, Charley. He might have told his clerk. I'll find out in the morning."

Wright stood up. He did not look pleased with the results of their conversation. After he left by the alley doorway, Fogarty locked up for the night, returned to his desk, and stood a moment in thought before blowing down the lamp mantle, stepping outside, and bolting the door.

There were only a few lights showing the length of Main Street. Behind town, out where there were residences, there were even fewer lights.

He listened to the echo of his own footfalls all the way up to the hotel. He halted on the porch to scan the area to the west where the big old bush flourished, shrugged, and went inside.

There was a hanging lamp midway along the dingy hallway. It provided excellent light. Someone had very recently trimmed the wick and cleaned the glass mantle.

For a moment after unlocking his own door he stood back looking southward, down where Miss Durning's room was, and to the rooms next to her room, one southward, one northward. He had no idea which one of those rooms belonged to the outlaw known as Ernest Macy.

His intention was to wake and rise before daybreak, and he managed it, but not quite as early as he'd wanted to.

When he left the hotel, walking across Main Street southward, the cafeman's roadside window suddenly glowed with light. Fogarty passed along without even looking in. He would not have seen anything; the cafeman would not unlock his front door for another hour and a half.

At the lower end of town where a straggling road came in from the east, Fogarty turned in that direction, did not even hesitate when he reached a small, nondescript half-log house, went up, and thumped on the door.

He had to knock several times before a wavering handheld lamp showed that someone was approaching the front window that was beside the front door.

Fogarty did not get a chance to speak. The thin man with tousled hair, sleep-puffy eyes, and receding chin pushed the lamp out as though he wanted to verify something and blurted words out in a wheezing manner. "What happened? The bank's been robbed! "

Fogarty smiled at Donner's clerk. "Nothing's happened at the bank, Ben. Mind if I come in for a few minutes? Sorry I got you out of bed."

Fogarty closed the door and stood with his back to it. Donner's clerk's threadbare old cotton bathrobe made him look even less impressive than he normally did. But he recovered quickly from the shock of seeing the town marshal on his doorstep and muttered something about coffee.

Fogarty declined. "I just got a couple of questions for you, then you can go back to bed. Ben, how did Mr. Donner know that money was counterfeit?"

The clerk ran a sleeve across his watering eyes before answering. "Marshal, how did you know that money was hid in his desk?"

"He told me."

"Well, did he tell you it was all right for us to talk about that money?"

Marshal Fogarty avoided a direct reply and said, "Ben, Mr. Donner's seen the light since he's been shot at twice."

The clerk nodded resignedly. "He sent me down to Mr. Dennis's store to pick up a pouch of money to be deposited at the bank. Mr. Dennis gave me the pouch and said business been real brisk the last couple of weeks. I told Mr. Donner that. He did what I've seen him do many times when all of a sudden there's lots of money circulating . . . "

"And?"

"He said about half that money was counterfeit. He put it in the hidey-hole in his desk and sent a couple of notes of it and a letter to the U.S. marshal's office in Denver. He told me neither one of us was to mention that to anyone. Not even to you."

Fogarty gazed steadily at the smaller man. "Who did you tell, Ben?"

The clerk straightened. "I never told a soul. I never talked about any of this until right now, with you. Not a damned word."

Fogarty slapped the clerk on the shoulder, made a little joke, and departed.

The sun was still somewhere down behind the most easterly rims, but the cafeman was not the only

84

merchant getting ready for the new day. Hank Dennis and his rickety old clerk with the black sleeve protectors were rolling barrels outside up against the store's big window. When Marshal Fogarty came along, Dennis straightened up. So did his clerk, but he simply bobbed his head at the lawman and went inside the store. Hank Dennis placed both hands flat against his sides and leaned far back as he said, "Good morning. There must be easier ways to make a livin' than storekeeping."

Fogarty offered no greeting and no sympathy for the merchant's sore back. He stepped close and said, "When you gave that money to Pete's clerk to be deposited, you told him business had been brisk lately."

Dennis nodded, his eyes widening.

"And how did you know some of that money was homemade?"

Now the storekeeper forgot about his backache. He looked around, saw no one close, and looked back as he was speaking. "Pete told me. The reason he told me was that when I went up there for my deposit slip, it showed a hundred dollars shy of what I'd put in the bag the clerk took up there. I went back to Pete's desk. I wasn't feelin' real friendly, Marshal. I leaned down on Pete's desk and told him if him or his clerk tried to steal from me, I'd break half the bones in their carcasses."

Fogarty's eyes showed a hint of amusement. "So, he showed you the counterfeit money?"

"Yes. That's how I knew."

"And who did you tell that Mr. Dormer had some homemade money up at the bank?"

Dennis fished out a large handkerchief and mopped off sweat, although it certainly had not warmed up yet. In fact, it was chilly on the east side of Main Street. He stuffed the handkerchief away and glanced past Marshal Fogarty.

The marshal reached and tapped Dennis's chest. "Who?"

Dennis's face twisted into a feeble little smile. "You probably never been in the store business, Joe, so you wouldn't know that when peddlers come around you set 'em down, give 'em a little coffee or whiskey, and they tell you the latest jokes. You understand. They are a storekeeper's best source of information from places like Denver and—"

"Hank, let me guess. The drummer told you the news from other towns, and you didn't want to seem to be livin' in a place where nothin' ever happened, so you told him Pete Donner had discovered counterfeit money in the greenbacks you deposited at the bank."

"Not exactly like that, Joe. It warn't that I wanted to impress on him that we have things happen in Sheridan . . ."

Fogarty smiled and did as he had done with the clerk: he gave Hank Dennis a light slap on the shoulder. Then he stepped off the duckboards heading for the jailhouse.

There was sunlight on his side of Main Street. On the opposite side shadows remained. Through the office window, Joe Fogarty watched Dennis and his old clerk arrange items for sale up against the front wall of the store. There had been a few complaints about that, mainly because the plank walk was not very wide as it was. Pedestrians had to edge around barrels of apples, one-horse planters, and the like, occasionally even having to step off the walkway if two people met going in opposite directions. Joe sympathized. In fact, he thought Hank was creating a deliberate nuisance, but as he had told the complainers, it was not up to the town marshal to do something, it was up to the town council, and unless enough people showed up at the monthly meetings to complain, nothing would be done.

Reg Lee arrived out front of the cafe from the southern end of town at about the same time Silas Browning and his corralyard foreman arrived from the opposite direction.

Fogarty stood at his office window watching. Breakfast time was the one period of the day when Sheridan's residents, at least the ones who were unmarried, congregated on time in front of the cafe. He continued to wait and watch, but neither Macy nor Booker appeared. If they had, it would have simplified the hell out of things for Marshal Fogarty.

THE INADVERTENT POSSE

HE WENT UP TO THE HOTEL TO ASK THE PROPRIETOR IF the pair of drummers were still in their rooms. He did not expect to receive a cooperative answer, and if he did not, he intended to take the proprietor with him to their closed doors and have him use his private key to open them.

Whether or not the lady detective and the deputy federal lawman thought they had sufficient evidence to nail the counterfeiters, Joe Fogarty was of the opinion that as town marshal he had enough information to take the pair of drummers down to the jailhouse for a talk.

The arrival of counterfeiters in his town, plus the attempted murder of Pete Donner—events that had occurred almost a week earlier—had opened up an affair that in Joe Fogarty's view had gone on about as long as it should.

But he did not find the proprietor. He encountered Elizabeth Durning in the hallway before he had a chance to look for the hotel owner, and she did as she had done at other times. She took the initiative by asking if Fogarty had talked with Charley Wright last night. When he told her that he had, she turned back, opened the door to her room, and waited for him to enter.

He turned back to face her in the center of the room. She closed the door, locked it, and pointed to the only chair in the room. He ignored the invitation to be seated. She asked what Charley had discovered at the tanyard shack. When he mentioned the heavy little bullion crates, she walked past him, sat on the chair he had declined to use, and spoke while looking up at him.

"Do you know a man named Cullen Dowd?"

He didn't. "I don't think so. The name isn't familiar."

She did not appear surprised. "He is the bearded man Macy and Booker met here in Sheridan."

"The freighter?"

"Yes. Those bullion boxes Charley saw last night were brought to Sheridan from Colorado Springs by Dowd."

Joe looked around. She had the only chair, so he perched on the edge of the bed. "How do you know that?"

She rose, crossed to the north wall, and took down a framed lithograph of a presidential inauguration. There was a small hole in the wall where the picture had been hanging. Joe did not rise as he thought she expected him to do. He simply nodded. "You could get a splinter in your ear," he told her dryly.

She rehung the picture, returned to the chair, and looked steadily at him. "What I'm having trouble with, Marshal, is Dowd's position. Of course he knew Macy and Booker up north, and I heard him tell Ernest Macy last night in Macy's room that it would require three weeks for him to go back up there, load up what they left behind, and return. Macy evidently knew this because he said it couldn't be helped. They hadn't had time to do more than hide the other crates. Dowd was a little worried that someone might be waiting up there to catch him loading the crates. Macy said all the federal marshal knew was that they had worked out of a house in Colorado Springs, and he could sit up there watching that house until the cows came home. The crates were miles away in an old abandoned barn. He gave Dowd a map so he can find them."

"So he's goin' back up there," Fogarty said. "All right. I'm not very interested in him, anyway. When he leaves town, I'm goin' to pick up his friends and have a little talk with them at the jailhouse. When he comes back, I'll have a nice dry cell for him, too."

The handsome woman gazed at the inaugural lithograph for a moment before speaking again. "Marshal, I think Cullen Dowd might be as important as Macy and Booker." She swung to face him again. "Have you wondered how Macy and Booker happened to decide Sheridan was a good place to start up again? I think the reason may be because Dowd told them it was. He has hauled freight down here. I heard him mention several names of local merchants. One was Pepperdine. Another was Dennis the storekeeper."

Fogarty's eyes widened. "That's how their homemade money got down here. Their freighter got it from them up north and passed some of it down here."

She smiled at Fogarty. "Very likely. But unless you can have that confirmed by Cullen Dowd . . ."

Fogarty got to his feet, glanced toward the north wall, and asked if either of the counterfeiters were in their rooms. She shook her head and would have spoken, but Fogarty was already moving toward the door. He stopped with a hand on the latch. "Unlock it, please."

She approached with the key in hand but made no move to obey. Instead she faced the marshal to say, "If you arrest them, and all you have to prove they are outlaws is a pair of sample cases with women's shoes in them and some revolvers, you won't be able to hold them, and they'll scatter like autumn leaves. Marshal, Charley and I have come too far, put up with too much inconvenience, to let that happen."

Fogarty looked down at her. "I'm not going to arrest them, lady, until I see what's inside those bullion boxes. But if there is anything like parts of money-making machinery in them, I'm going to lock them up and feed the keys to a turkey." He paused, took the key from her hand, unlocked the door, and handed back the key with a little smile. "I've read a couple of accounts how the Pinkertons work. It made interestin' reading, and all this backing and filling about evidence and the like might be real important in Denver, but it sure as hell isn't in Sheridan."

He walked out, closed the door after himself, and did not look back until he was out on the porch. Then he paused, half expecting her to come after him. If she did, she got out there too late. Fogarty was on his way to the jailhouse. He had no intention of bracing whoever might be inside the tanyard shack without being fully prepared. If all three men were in there, they would probably be armed. There was no six-gun in the world, not even a double-action one, that could successfully stand up to three other six-guns. The only weapon capable of doing that was a sawed-off shotgun. There were three of them in the jailhouse wall rack.

Fogarty was unlocking the chain that ran through all the trigger guards of his racked weapons when Hugh Pepperdine walked in, stopped stone still, and watched him select a scattergun. As Fogarty was restringing and locking the chain, Pepperdine said, "You know who tried to kill Pete Donner?"

Fogarty went to his desk to rummage for the box containing shotgun shells. "I don't know who tried to shoot Pete."

Pepperdine did not accept that curt dismissal. "Well, it's got to be somethin' like that because turkey season ain't here yet."

Fogarty finished putting shotgun shells in a pocket and looked up. "Somethin' I can do for you?"

"Yeah, there is. Silas owed me for patching some old harness." As Pepperdine said this, he groped in a trouser pocket until he found what he was seeking and held it out toward Fogarty. "He come in an hour or so ago, took his harness, and give me this to settle the bill."

Fogarty looked at the outstretched hand with the crumpled greenback in it, put down his scattergun, and took the note. He sat down at the desk, tipped back his hat, and studied the numbers that were the only thing on the money he thought might have been inscribed by hand.

Hugh walked over, waited patiently, then reached and without a word turned the greenback over. "See the federal eagle, Joe? It's got no feet."

Fogarty looked up. "How did you happen to notice that?"

Pepperdine was shifting his cud from one cheek to the other and could not answer until this had been completed. Then he said, "I put it in my money drawer. Later, when I figured I'd go over to the saloon for somethin' cool, I grabbed it, dropped it, an' when I bent down to pick it up—by golly, that's the first federal saddle blanket I ever saw where the eagle didn't have no claws an' no feet."

Fogarty put the bill in a drawer as he rose. "I'll keep it for now, if you don't mind." He was reaching for the shotgun when Pepperdine protested. "Dang it all, Joe, I put in two full days sewin' on that harness. I'll take it up yonder and make old Silas eat it."

Fogarty sighed, fished for a note from his own pocket, and handed it to the harnessmaker. As Pepperdine accepted it, he scowled. "You don't suppose old Silas is turning to makin' counterfeit money, do you? At his age?"

Fogarty was moving toward the door with the scattergun in the crook of one arm as he replied, "Don't say a word to Silas, and close the door when you leave."

He probably would not have stopped at the corralyard if Jack Carpenter hadn't hailed him from the gateway. Carpenter was a tactful individual. He acted as though the marshal was not carrying a sawed-off shotgun when he said, "I thought that pretty lady with the curly hair an' blue eyes was goin' on south. I been waitin' for her to show up on one of my runs." Jack jutted his jaw. "I just saw her walkin' toward the lower end of town. Maybe she liked Sheridan enough to settle in. You reckon?"

Fogarty eyed the coach driver in silence for a moment before saying, "You're a married man."

Carpenter did not deny that. "Yes, sir, for a fact, but that don't mean I went blind, too."

Silas Browning came scuffing across the yard. Fogarty waited until he was close, then put a question to him. "Do you have any particular freighters you favor for heavy haulin', Silas?"

Browning looked up with testy eyes. "I use whichever freighter is around when I need one. Why?"

"Do you ever use one named Dowd?"

"Cullen Dowd? Lots of times. He's been showin' up in Sheridan for must be close to a year by now. What's wrong with him?"

"Has he hauled anything for you lately?"

"Just the other way around. Jack brought in some light freight for him from down south. Paper, warn't it, Jack?"

Carpenter nodded. "Three packages of paper. Maybe we're goin' to have a regular newspaper."

Fogarty was not diverted. "Dowd paid you for the haul, Silas?"

"Of course he paid me. I ain't in the charity business . . . Why all the questions, Marshal?"

Fogarty leaned, smiled, and pinched the old man's cheek, then stepped back before the sputtering arrived. Silas was still gesticulating and cursing after Marshal Fogarty had crossed the road. Jack Carpenter had a bulging thick vein in the side of his neck, and his face was red from his struggle to keep from laughing.

Old Silas went stamping back into the yard, mad as a wet hen.

McGregor was sitting on a bench in front of his gun shop. He had witnessed the humiliation of Silas Browning and was very close to smiling when Marshal Fogarty came along. One reason his smile did not mature was that short-barreled murder gun Joe was carrying. Sawed-off shotguns were good for nothing except close-range killing, and they were about as good a weapon as a man could have for that.

McGregor greeted the lawman with a dry remark. "Be

careful with that thing. I've seen one of 'em cut a oak barrel plumb in two from twenty feet . . . Joe?"

Fogarty stopped. "What?"

"Just wanted to tell you me'n Hugh was real grateful for that bottle."

"You're welcome."

"Joe . . . "

"Now what?"

"Look yonder. Hugh's comin' wearin' his belt gun and carryin' his Winchester."

When Fogarty twisted to look across the road, McGregor rose and disappeared inside his shop. Fogarty did not miss him because he was waiting for the harnessmaker. "Where do you think you're goin' with those guns?" he asked.

Pepperdine beamed a broad smile. "Wherever you're goin' with that gun."

Fogarty's neck swelled. "You're not goin' to do any such a thing. You stay here. Stay clean away from me. You understand?"

Hugh didn't answer. McGregor did from the doorway of his shop. He was also wearing a shell belt and a belt gun, and he was holding a freshly blued Winchester saddle gun in his hands. "We're goin' with you, so you might as well get used to it. Now tell me, Marshal, where are we going?"

Fogarty glared. It did no good. He growled. That had no effect on either of the old men. He looked around, saw several people on the opposite plank walk staring, and faced forward again. "We're goin' up to the tanyard, an' don't either one of you draw a six-gun nor cock a carbine while you're behind me."

He was already moving when Hugh said, "The tannery? You're goin' after Jim Young with a

94

scattergun? Joe, you don't need a gun to take Jim in tow. He's the most harmless feller I—"

"We're not goin' after Jim. We're goin' out back to that shed behind his tanning works." Fogarty paused to look back. "There could be three men in the shed. If they're armed, and sure as hell they are, you two fan off on both sides of me but don't raise a gun unless I run into trouble with them."

McGregor and Pepperdine subsided. They marched in Fogarty's wake all the way up to the log fence that formed the front of Jim Young's rather long, deep piece of tanyard property. They followed Fogarty inside and halted only when Jim Young emerged from a small building that gave off unpleasant odors and whose doorway was a point of rendezvous for hundreds of blue-tailed flies.

Jim usually smiled. This time, as he dried his hands on a filthy old towel, he stared at the guns more than at the men bearing them. Marshal Fogarty took him to one side and asked if anyone was in the little shed out back.

Young did not know. "I been inside washin' down hides an' skivin' off hair all morning. They could be over there. For all I know, Marshal, they could be anywhere. I did see that husky feller with the beard over here before breakfast this morning, if that's any help to you."

Fogarty pushed up a smile even though he was directly facing toward the distant shack. "We're obliged, Jim. Go on back to your work. I don't know that there'll be any trouble, but if there is, you stay inside and keep your head down."

The somewhat dense tanner scowled. "Trouble? You mean with Mr. Booker an' Mr. Macy? Marshal, them's as nice a pair of gents as you'd ever meet."

Fogarty turned his smile toward Young. "Sure they

95

are. All the same, keep your head down. Hugh, James, start fannin' out."

As Pepperdine moved to comply, he spoke from the corner of his mouth. "You're goin' to look almighty foolish, Marshal, if that shack is empty."

HOW TO LOSE
WHILE WINNING

THE SHACK WASN'T EMPTY. WHEN JOE FOGARTY gripped the latch, very gently squeezed it enough to raise the inner *tranca*, then hurled his weight against it, nearly tearing the door from its hinges, the two men who were leaning over something near the center of the room jerked upright and whirled.

Marshal Fogarty cocked his shotgun.

The shorter of the occupants, who was swarthy and thickly built, said, "Don't do anythin' rash, Marshal. We're not goin' to buck you."

Both the drummers were looking straight at the cocked gun that was no more than fifteen feet from them. Fogarty wigwagged with the gun barrel. "Move aside."

They moved. Both the steel-reinforced boxes had been opened. One contained what appeared to be some kind of fine hand tools. The other box was half full of new money, which was bound by red yarn.

Joe looked at Macy and Booker. "Where's Dowd?"

"He ain't here," the swarthy man said, watching Fogarty closely. "What d'you think you're doing? We got a right to be in here."

"Yeah. Are those engraving tools in the box nearest your partner?"

Macy looked around, then back. "Sure. Sometimes when I peddle weapons, someone'll want their names on 'em. Bill here is a real good engraver."

Fogarty gave an order. "Hold your coats open. Now, then, drop those pistols. Use your left hands and be awful damned careful."

The guns looked new; none of the bluing had been worn off them. They were both Lightning Colts. Fogarty considered the men who had dropped them. "Now pull up your britches legs, an' after that shed those coats."

Macy looked pained. "Neither one of us carries a belly gun."

"Do it, anyway," replied Fogarty, and after being obeyed, this time he eased down the hammer of his weapon and let the gun hang at his side as he stepped closer to examine the contents of the boxes. The small hand tools could indeed have been engraving instruments—Fogarty was not familiar with tools of that kind—but the packets of yarn-wrapped money in the other box had never been in circulation. When considered in conjunction with the contents of the first box, plus what he already knew about his prisoners, he would have bet a ton of new money he was looking at thousands of counterfeit dollars, which were ready to be put into circulation.

Someone hailed the shed from outside. Fogarty moved back to the door and called back, "Come on in."

Macy and Booker looked indifferently at the harnessmaker and the gunsmith when they appeared. Their interest was in Marshal Fogarty, who knelt between the bullion boxes, removed a packet of greenbacks, and untied it. Because the light in the center of the room was inadequate for his purpose, he retreated to the doorway, where sunshine made it possible for him

97

to detect the same kind of hand-inscribed serial numbers he had found on the other counterfeit currency.

Macy and Booker watched everything he did. When he moved back toward them in the middle of the shed, Macy said, "Somethin' wrong with it, Marshal? A storekeeper over in Idaho gave me that money in payment for an order of double-action Colt pistols."

Fogarty was folding the homemade greenbacks when he smiled at the swarthy man. "Sure he did." Fogarty pocketed the notes, still smiling. "He must have bought a lot of those little guns. I have more of this same kind of money down at my office. Looks to me like the same feller wrote the numbers on all of it. But there was something else. Maybe you didn't notice, or maybe it couldn't be helped, but at least one of your bills missed havin' the feet and claws on the eagle. I've got that one, too."

Fogarty gestured. "Pick up your coats, gents. Leave the guns lie. Now, then, walk out of here ahead of me. Don't walk fast. Don't even think about makin' a break. My friends here are both dead shots. They'll be right behind you."

Fogarty waited until the outlaws were being herded away before stepping back inside, closing the box with the money in it, hoisting it to his shoulder, and striking out after Hugh and James. The procession southward and across the road in the direction of the jailhouse caused people on both sidewalks, as well as on horseback and on buggy and wagon seats, to gape.

Hugh Pepperdine seemed to enjoy being the center of attention. McGregor didn't. He did not enjoy any kind of notoriety. Marshal Fogarty ignored it. While the federal law and the Pinkerton lady were palavering somewhere about the technicalities of proper legal procedure, Fogarty had caught the counterfeiters with evidence to hell and back right beside them. That was all that mattered to him.

When the small procession disappeared inside the jailhouse, roadway traffic returned to normal, except, of course, that now there was something infinitely more exciting to talk about than the weather.

McGregor would have lingered in Fogarty's office, but Pepperdine nudged him and led the way outside. James was indignant. "After we helped him round them up, we had a right to find out what it was all about."

"It was about counterfeit money," the taller, leaner man said. "You saw it in the box. You saw Joe take them notes to the light. An' we got businesses to run."

As they were walking northward, the gunsmith abruptly said, "Counterfeit money! Maybe it's all over town, Hugh."

Pepperdine did not slacken stride or look at his companion. "And what difference would that make? You give some to me, I give it to someone else, and they pass it along to someone else on down the line. Hell, Silas give me some of it. One of the notes with the eagle on the back—well, the eagle didn't have no feet."

"What did you do with it?"

"Showed it to Joe. He took it for evidence or something, and give me a good note for it. You see?"

When they parted, McGregor stepped down into the roadway still looking worried, but not as much so as before.

At the jailhouse office, neither Booker nor Macy looked worried as they watched Marshal Fogarty place the bullion box atop his desk, open it, and sift through the little yarn-wrapped packets. When he finally closed the box and put it behind his chair, William Booker smiled beguilingly. "That Idaho storekeeper sure roped Ernie in, didn't he? Bought all those little guns with counterfeit money."

Fogarty sat down, ignored Booker, and gazed steadily at the shorter, darker man. "Where are the presses you print the money on?"

Macy's gaze back at Joe Fogarty was stone-steady. "You think we made that money?"

"Yes, sir, I do."

Macy's dark eyes glowed sardonically. "Prove it, Marshal. Like you said—where are the presses and where are the engraved plates counterfeiters use with their presses?"

Fogarty had just learned something about homemade money. It was made from engraved plates. He allowed an interval of silence to pass before he said, "Want me to guess where the equipment is you use to make money with?"

Macy's faintly sardonic expression lingered. He nodded his head without speaking or taking his gaze off Fogarty.

Fogarty paused again. This time he leaned back in his chair, too. "In crates in an old abandoned barn up near Colorado Springs."

Macy's expression changed only to the extent that his gaze on Fogarty hardened, but William Booker's mouth dropped open.

Fogarty fished for his tobacco sack and papers. While he was making a smoke, he said, "Want to hear a little more, gents? Your friend with the whiskers passed some of that fake money over at the general store. The storekeeper put it in the bank, and Pete Donner found out it was counterfeit. You found out from the storekeeper that the banker had the money and knew it

100

was fake. You tried to kill him so's the word would not spread. I know how you did it."

Fogarty lit up and trickled smoke. "When you knew the banker wasn't dead, you slipped under the window at Doc Pohl's place and tried again." He smiled straight at Ernest Macy. "You missed again. You didn't know that, did you? Donner was in the outhouse out back. What you shot was his lumpy blankets. Shot 'em twice. Shootin' in the dark can cause a man to make mistakes like that."

Fogarty rocked forward, rested both elbows on the desk, and studied Ernest Macy, who was staring at him with an expressionless face. Fogarty stubbed out his smoke in the smashed-flat tomato can.

He didn't know the freighter, but he knew William Booker sufficiently well to believe that he had neither the grit nor the brains to be the organizer or the leader of the counterfeiting organization, and that left the swarthy, stocky man who was sitting like a stone statue staring at him.

He ignored Booker. "You got any questions, Mr. Macy? I can answer most of them."

The dark man's expression did not change. He barely parted his lips when he said, "You don't have a damned bit of proof about any of this."

Fogarty barely inclined his head. "The box behind me will do for openers. Those engraving tools up in the shed will help. And there's the storekeeper who remembered Dowd giving him that homemade money. But best of all, you boys rode stages all the way from Denver down to Sheridan in the company of a deputy U.S. marshal and a Pinkerton detective. They were on your trail before you left Denver."

William Booker shot a frightened look at his

101

companion, but Macy ignored it. He was regarding Joe Fogarty without showing anything on his face. "Let me tell you something about the law, Marshal. Everything you've said so far don't fit what is required to get a conviction in a court. Bill an' I are traveling salesmen. We can prove it. We got contracts with wholesalers. We get orders an' we sell their merchandise. We can prove every damned bit of it, too. All you can prove is that you busted into that shed where we had just discovered that a storekeeper over in Idaho paid me with counterfeit money. We'll swear to that under oath."

Fogarty was silent for a long time. He did not doubt that he could bring them to court, nor that he had enough evidence to impress one of the circuit-riding judges who passed through from time to time, but he had been learning something about Ernest Macy, or whatever his name was, since they had entered the jailhouse.

Macy was as different from his partner as night was from day. Booker would cave in. He might be a talented engraver, but he did not have a ramrod up his back like Macy had.

Fogarty sat there grudgingly beginning to respect his adversary. If he got Macy sent to prison, he was going to earn it every step of the way. He said, "It'll take your friend the freighter about a month to get up yonder, find those boxes, and get back down here. I can warn the U.S. marshal in Denver he's comin', and I can tell the marshal where he'll be. It shouldn't be very hard for him to have that barn surrounded when your friend loads the boxes."

Macy had been surprised and shocked, but he was over that by now. He, too, had learned a little respect; the big town marshal he had thought was just another cowtown lawman, long on brawn and maybe gunmanship and short on everything else, had been proving himself to be something very different.

But Macy had been in scrapes with the law all his adult life. He had survived every such encounter up to now, and was confident he would survive this encounter. But one thing was glaringly clear: All his careful planning in the selection of Sheridan as his new base of operations was shot to pieces.

Fogarty jarred him out of his bitter thoughts by mentioning something Macy hadn't had the time to think much about. "Attempted murder is something I've had experience with. You're lucky you missed, otherwise they'd have hanged you. I have the slug that was taken out of the banker. Our local gunsmith shaped it back up. It came from one of your Lightning Colts. The gunsmith is real good at comparin' slugs from the same gun. Mr. Macy, he's helped me get some real good convictions."

This time the swarthy man's reaction was different. He straightened up, glared, and said, "You'll never in this world prove I shot Donner."

Joe smiled slyly. "Fine. If I don't, why, then I expect you'll get off with maybe fifteen years in prison and I'll prove by comparison that Mr. Booker did it."

The heretofore silent counterfeiterer made a little throaty gasp. He was sweating. He probably would have protested, but Macy reached with a powerful set of fingers and clamped down on his arm. Booker flinched in pain, and Macy addressed Joe Fogarty. "You go right ahead and do your damnedest, Marshal . . . I got to say you sure surprised me. But that's not goin' to count for a damn."

If Macy had been ready to say more, he did not have

the opportunity. A large, red-faced man burst in from the roadway door looking badly upset and sweaty. A strong tanyard odor entered with him.

Joe Fogarty looked around irritably. "Jim, not right now."

The tanner ignored that to blurt out words in a rush. "Marshal, I got to tell you. He sent me to tell you."

Fogarty's stomach sank. He had never seen Jim Young so agitated before. "Tell me what?"

"He's got 'em both. The lady an' the feller who dungs out for Mr. Lee down at the livery barn."

"Who's got them?"

"I don't know his name. The feller I told you I saw at the shack early this morning. He brought the lady and that cowboy up to the shed. I watched 'em go inside. When they come out, he saw me standin' in the yard and yelled out. His friends wasn't in there. He told me if I lied to him he'd shoot me. I told him you'n Hugh'n James snuck in there and took his friends down here, an' you toted one of those bullion boxes along."

Fogarty looked at Macy and Booker. The dark man was staring at Jim Young exultantly. William Booker was white to the hairline, also staring at the tanner.

Fogarty stood up slowly. "What did he send you to tell me, Jim?"

"Well, he cussed a lot. I thought he'd shoot me sure as hell."

"Jim—what did he send you down here to tell me!"

"Well, that he'd be watchin' an' if he didn't see them two gents walk out of here, he was goin' to gut-shoot the lady an' the livery-barn hostler. Marshal, he ain't jokin'; he means it."

FIGURING THINGS OUT

FOGARTY WAS STARING AT THE DESK TOP WHEN THE tanner said, "What'll I tell him? He's waitin' for me up there."

Before Fogarty could speak, the swarthy man said, "Tell him we'll be along. Tell him to tie up his prisoners, an' get three good horses."

Jim Young left, and Joe Fogarty looked at the closed roadway door, then sat back down. Macy showed an exultant smile. "All your snoopin' and schemin' shot to hell, Marshal. Let me tell you somethin' about Cullen Dowd. He spent eleven years in prison for train robbery and a killing. If you're figuring some way to talk your way around him, I can tell you he'll do exactly as he said unless Bill and I walk out of here. There's somethin' else you ought to know about Cullen: He's not a patient man. I'd guess it'll take him maybe fifteen minutes to get those horses. After that we'd better be walkin' up the roadway."

Fogarty leaned back in his chair looking at the ceiling. He knew now what he should have done. He should have locked Macy and his partner in a cell and gone after the freighter.

It was his own damned fault. He'd gone up there with his shotgun like a bull in a china closet. He winced at the thought of what the Pinkerton lady would say—if she lived to say anything.

He eased the chair forward and gazed at his prisoners. Macy wasn't quite smiling, but his stare at Fogarty had gallows humor in it. "Fifteen minutes," he murmured.

Booker had recovered a little color, but he remained visibly apprehensive as he waited for the lawman to speak. It was a fairly long wait.

"You won't get ten miles, Macy."

The outlaw's sardonic gaze brightened a little. "We'll get ten times that far, an' you won't be after us. We'll take the lady and the cowboy with us."

"On three horses?"

"No. Cullen will get three horses for Bill an' me an' him. When I get up to the tanyard, we'll get two more horses. Cullen's got killing in mind. I know how he thinks. But I don't think that way. The cowboy and the lady . . ." Macy snapped off the last word with his eyes widening. "Is that who they are: a deputy U.S. marshal and a Pinkerton detective?" When Fogarty did not answer, the swarthy man slapped his leg. "Bill, you were wrong. Remember what you said about her on the ride down here? That she was too pretty to be travelin' alone?"

Booker did not reply. He was wiping off sweat with a limp handkerchief.

Macy faced the desk again. "Time is passing, Marshal. Cullen will be peeking down the road from up there."

Fogarty's ability to reach a swift decision had been impaired by what had suddenly turned into a nightmare. But he made a frantic effort to find an alternative, anyway. He was desperate enough to consider locking up his prisoners, then leaving the jailhouse by the back alley to try to sneak up within shooting distance of the tanyard.

Macy repeated his earlier statement. "Time is passing. You're goin' to sit there until those folks get killed. It'll happen as sure as I'm talkin' to you. If you knew Cullen as well as I do, you'd know it's the gospel truth."

Fogarty ran bent fingers through his hair, dropped his hat back down, and stood up.

106

Macy hadn't taken his eyes off him. "You better use your head, Marshal. If you let those people get killed up there, do you think folks here in Sheridan will want you around? You'll be lucky if they don't lynch you. Marshal? You're not the first lawman who got skunked, an' you won't be the last. Don't take it so hard. What the hell—losin' one batch of prisoners isn't somethin' you can't make up for in the years ahead . . . Well? You only got about five minutes left."

Fogarty went to the roadway door, opened it, and looked toward the upper end of town. Everywhere else Sheridan was going about its normal business, but the tanyard with its old broken gate was as quiet and still as a graveyard. He turned back. "Come over here, you two."

Macy was on his feet instantly. William Booker also rose, but he hung back when his partner crossed to the doorway.

Fogarty looked down at the shorter man. Not a word passed between them until Fogarty jerked his head for the outlaws to walk out into the roadway, then Macy smiled at him. "We'll never meet again, but I'll remember you . . . Bill, come along."

Booker hesitated. "What about the money?"

Macy reddened. "Leave it. Let the marshal here pass it. We'll get set up somewhere and make more. Dammit, come along!"

Booker edged around the formidable, bitter-faced lawman to follow his partner out of the jailhouse. There were people on both sides of the road. There were women with net shopping bags on their arms, and men heading for the cafe. It wasn't dinnertime yet, but it was close enough, especially for men who made their living by hard manual labor.

107

A light spring wagon was approaching the general store. It had some cow outfit's brand burned into the wood below the seat. A pair of range riders were passing southward at a steady walk. Fogarty watched his prisoners cross the road and turn northward. It was like having a foot in two worlds, one normal, one totally abnormal.

He closed the door, took a booted Winchester and his coat, and left the building by the back-alley door. On his way southward to the livery barn he did not hasten. Uppermost in his mind was something Macy had repeatedly warned him about: Cullen Dowd was a killer.

If he saw Fogarty down their back trail, he might kill Charley Wright and Elizabeth Durning. He might not, too, since they were essential if the outlaws were to escape. But it was not a choice Joe Fogarty wanted to put to a test.

Reg Lee was sitting sprawled in an old chair inside the runway chewing a blade of timothy hay when Fogarty came through from out back. Reg had plenty of time to study the marshal's expression. He leaned forward and spoke around the drooping hay stalk. "Somebody's in trouble, an' you're goin' to miss dinner." He stood up. "I'll get your horse." As an afterthought the liveryman added a little more. "I been in this business a long time, I've had just about every kind of man work for me. I got to the place where I could just about tell what they'd amount to by lookin' at them. But that damned cowboy I hired for nightman fooled me real good. I took a shine to him, so I let him work days, and you know what? He ain't here. He did the chores this morning, then he upped and disappeared." Lee was taking down a lead shank when he finished his diatribe. "When he walks through the

108

door, I'm goin' to fire him so fast he won't have time to blink."

Fogarty leaned the booted saddle gun aside and entered the combination office and harness room for his outfit. As he was emerging, Reg appeared leading his horse. "If they ain't drunks or fugitives, they're shiftless."

Fogarty cuffed the horse, then draped the blanket and was reaching for the saddle when the liveryman spoke again, still irritated by the absence of his dayman. "You haven't seen him, have you?"

Fogarty grunted the saddle up as he replied, "No."

They finished with the horse in silence, but when Fogarty started for the back alley, Reg walked beside the led horse. "You're not too talkative this morning, Marshal."

"Got no reason to be," Fogarty replied, turned his animal, and swung across leather.

Reg frowned up at him. "Had breakfast?" he asked, and got a curt shake of the head as Fogarty reined northward.

Lee stood out there watching the lawman's progress. He scratched his head, went back up to his harness room, got his hat, and walked briskly northward up Main Street.

He did not expect to find his missing hostler at the cafe, but he looked in, anyway. Nor did he expect to find him at the saloon, nor did he, but when he poked his head past the spindle doors, three townsmen looked up from the bar, and one of them, the one wearing the brocaded vest, spoke. "Come on over here. We was just discussin' somethin' that might interest you."

Reg dutifully crossed to the bar. Hugh Pepperdine, the tallest of them, looked down his nose at the liveryman. "We can't find the marshal."

Lee resolved that instantly. "He just left town on horseback up the west-side alley." Reg looked at the serious faces of the saloonman, the gunsmith, and the harnessmaker, then leaned on the bar as he said, "Somethin' was sure eatin' him. An' he had a saddle gun along. Missed breakfast, too. Didn't hardly act civil." Reg looked from face to face. "Is somethin' wrong?"

No one answered the question, but all three men exchanged a look before McGregor spoke in his crisp, minimal manner. "He took two fellers prisoner in that old shed up in back of Jim's tanyard. Hugh an' I was with him. We helped him take them down to the jailhouse along with a box of homemade money and some engravin' tools. Well, Joe's not at the jailhouse, and neither are those two fellers."

Reg was interested. "Who was they?"

"A pair of traveling peddlers. At least that's what they passed theirselves off as bein' around town. But they was counterfeiters."

Silence settled. This was the point where Morton, McGregor, and Pepperdine had ended their earlier discussion. Reg Lee asked if anyone had seen his dayman. No one had, but McGregor had seen something else: That lady with the sturdy build and the short curly hair had walked all the way down to the livery barn and entered.

Reg scowled. "When? Hell, I got to work an hour ago and there wasn't no lady there. And no hostler. Holy hell, you don't suppose they ran off together?"

McGregor looked annoyed. "Her, run off with a livery-barn tout? She could hitch up with a general or a governor—"

"Or an evil-minded old gunsmith," Pepperdine said, as he braced to jump sideways in case James swung at him. But James had suddenly thought of something. "Those two drummers run with a whiskered feller, husky sort who looks like a freighter. Maybe we can find him."

Pepperdine had a different idea. "Let's go up to the tanyard. Maybe Marshal Fogarty went back up there. Jim would know. Remember, James, he left one of those bullion crates in the shed along with the guns he made those two drummers drop."

McGregor looked stonily from his friend to Rusty Morton. "Fetch a bottle. I know, it's too early. Fetch a bottle, anyway. I'm goin' to get a headache. Somethin's goin' on. Hugh, remember how nasty Joe was to us when we offered to help him this morning? Well, seems he acted the same way with Reg. That's not Joe Fogarty's way . . . Rusty, what the hell are you waitin' for?" Morton hastened after the bottle and the little glasses. In his absence McGregor went on speaking.

"Jim would know if he went back up there." McGregor scowled at the floor, forgot the liveryman was standing there, and spoke directly to his old friend. "Hugh, can you smell tripe cooking?"

Pepperdine ignored the barman's return with their refreshment. "I think so. But why'n hell was Joe so damned secretive?"

Morton filled their glasses, set the bottle down hard to attract their attention, and watched them reach for their jolts. He did not say a word until McGregor pulled forth a capacious leather coin purse, unlatched it, and, pushing upward from the bottom with one hand, groped inside for several silver coins. Every man standing there had seen James McGregor go through this ritual many

111

times. He would push and grope and look around until someone got impatient and tossed coins atop the bar, then he would methodically snap his purse and return it to his pocket without a word.

Rusty said, "On the house, James." All three of them watched McGregor relatch his purse and stow it away without looking at any of them. Pepperdine had been saying for years that the only thing tighter than the bark on a tree was James McGregor.

"We're not goin' to know any more until we find either that freighter or Jim Young," the gunsmith said, and pushed away from the bar.

As the three men were leaving his saloon, Morton called after them, "Want me to round up the town possemen?"

McGregor shook his head without answering and led the way northward.

The morning was beautifully flawless and warm. Only when they were within fifty yards of the tannery was the fragile fragrance of wildflowers replaced by a more down-to-earth aroma and flies.

They found the big, somewhat childlike tanner in the shed where the blue-tailed flies were thickest. He dried off both hands and arms as he walked forth to meet them. He did not allow them time to ask their questions. His forehead creased into two deep lines as he said, "There wasn't nothin' I could do. He would have shot me. I thought he was goin' to, anyway. I know they stole them horses."

Hugh, Reg, and James stared at the hulking younger man. Reg said, "Who was goin' to shoot you?"

"The one called Cullen. The freighter with the beard. It was him kept the lady and that cowboy facin' the wall when he told me to go down to the jailhouse an' tell Mr.

112

Fogarty he would gut-shoot the lady and the cowboy if Mr. Fogarty didn't let them two partners of his, the men named Booker an' Macy, walk out of the jailhouse an' come up here."

All the starch went out of Pepperdine and McGregor. Reg Lee was regarding Jim Young quizzically. "Did you know the cowboy?" Young shook his head. "Was he sort of lean, about as tall as Hugh, and sort of leathery-skinned, maybe about your age?"

Jim almost smiled at the liveryman. "That's him. Did you know him?"

"He dunged out for me."

"Him an' the lady knew each other real well. It seemed to me they did, anyway."

McGregor turned toward the harnessmaker. "They used the lady an' the cowboy to get Macy and Booker free." He fumed back toward Jim Young. "They stole some horses?"

"Five head. The freighter done that. I don't know where he got 'em, but maybe at some tie-rack because they was already saddled and bridled. Mr. McGregor, someone's goin' to be mad as hell when they come lookin' for their animals."

"They took the lady an' the cowboy with them?"

"Yes, sir," Young replied, and pointed. "They been gone maybe an hour. Northward. They took the little box with them, too. The one in the shed out back that had those hand tools in it."

Reg Lee blew out a big breath. "An' now we know why Joe Fogarty was so cranky an' why he left town with a saddle gun. James?"

"What?"

"I'd better go tell Rusty to round up the town possemen."

113

Pepperdine spoke up. "Just let that hang an' rattle for now. They didn't take the lady an' the cowboy because they wanted company. They took 'em along to make damned certain Fogarty an' the rest of us wouldn't make a run on them. Hostages sure as hell."

McGregor stood lost in thought for a while, then he thanked the tanner for his help, led his companions back down to where there were fewer flies, halted, and said, "If they keep northward, they're crossin' open country all the way to the mountains. They'll see anyone shaggin' after them from a hell of a distance."

The liveryman thought he had the answer to that. "We can wait until evening."

McGregor looked annoyed again. "They'll reach the mountains by then. Did you ever try to find a needle in a haystack—in the dark?"

Hugh Pepperdine batted at a fly with one hand. "James, no one pays any attention to a stagecoach goin' up the road. There is a northbound every afternoon or early evening. Besides, the last time we got roped into somethin' like this, couldn't neither one of us set down without a pillow for a week."

McGregor did not speak for a long while. A saddle horse provided maneuverability. A stagecoach not only could not travel over rough country very well, but it could only take them to where they would have to leave it to get in front of the fleeing people; then they would be on foot.

He said, "I need another drink."

They trooped back to Morton's place.

PREPARING THE AMBUSH

SILAS BROWNING SNIFFED SUSPICIOUSLY. FOR ONE THING, this was the first time the gunsmith, the harnessmaker, and the liveryman had ever come into his yard together to pay for seats on the northbound stage, all armed, and all smelling of whiskey.

He took their money. If Señor Satan had been with them, complete with horns, pitchfork, and tail, Silas would have taken his money, too, hot though it might be, but he glared at them. Behind him a coach was being readied for the road and Jack Carpenter was coming from the bunkhouse along the back wall. "Just goin' for a ride, are you?" Silas asked sourly.

McGregor fixed old Browning with his pale gaze when he answered. "I've rode your coaches for years an' I've never heard you ask a question like that before. Gettin' nosy along with bein' cranky, are you?"

Silas stamped angrily toward the office door for his hat and clipboard. Whiskey drinkers, he told himself. Whiskey-drinking, evil old men. Well, they'd be in good company: Jack Carpenter was another one.

Carpenter was carrying his coat. He would not need it until after sundown. He also had his smoke-tanned gauntlets. As he passed the coach, he flung the coat into the boot of the high seat and continued forward, pulling on the gloves. He smiled at the three armed townsmen. "You boys look like the James gang with them guns. You goin' up-country with me?"

"Yeah."

"Fine. I hope one of you brought a bottle along."

McGregor ignored that. "How long before we roll?"

115

By this time Carpenter was beginning to sense the townsmen were not in a very good mood. "As soon as they put the animals on the pole and toss some light freight into the rear boot. Somethin' wrong?"

"Seems like that. Those drummers you brought to town a week or so back taken Reg's dayman and that pretty lady with the curly hair for hostages, and stole enough horses for the lot of them to head north."

Carpenter looked slowly from face to face before speaking. "That pretty lady with them real blue eyes? And Reg's hostler? What in hell for?"

"Because they're counterfeiters. Joe left town a while back on horseback lookin' for them."

Carpenter gave each gauntlet an extra tug before saying, "That pretty lady and the hostler are counterfeiters?"

The liveryman rolled his eyes. "No, dammit. Them two traveling peddlers are counterfeiters."

Carpenter nodded, but it was clear he was confused about all this. As he was turning away he said, "I'll hurry things up a little."

There were no other passengers. By the time several bulky but light-weight crates had been loaded in the boot, the horses were hitched, and Jack was ready to swarm up to his high seat, old Silas had emerged from his office, clipboard in hand and wearing his oversized hat. What the significance of the hat was had been a matter of local conjecture for years, but Silas had never volunteered any information and no one had ever asked him about it, so the small, wizened old man beneath the big hat with its outsized brim, grotesque though he looked, was accepted as one of the anomalies of Sheridan.

But it made it hard to take Silas seriously when he

116

was beneath that hat, as he now was as he approached the waiting townsmen to ask them a question.

"This ain't town-possemen business, is it? Because if it is, I don't want one of my stages used in somethin' that might get a horse shot or a wheel busted."

Hugh Pepperdine smiled. "If it was possemen business, there'd be four or five more of us."

Old Silas was not entirely appeased. He pointed. "You got guns. I never seen any of you takin' a coach out of town carryin' guns before."

Carpenter whistled his hitch into movement. Silas and the townsmen had to move aside. Jack stopped beside them and jerked his head for the armed men to get inside. Then he spoke to the stationmaster. "If that pretty lady's up the road, we'll find her." He whistled his horses into movement again, aimed for the opposite plank walk, and, inches before his leaders struck it, swung them to their left so that the coach's wheel hubs would clear the corralyard gateposts.

Silas followed the rig past the gates and stood out there peering perplexedly from beneath his hat brim as the northbound straightened out, aiming for the open country beyond Sheridan's northerly limits. One of the hostlers also walked out to watch. He was drying both hands on a greasy old flour sack when Silas said, "A pretty lady? Sam, was Jack drinkin' in the bunkhouse again?"

The yardman continued using the flour sack as he replied, "I don't know, Mr. Browning. I haven't been back there since breakfast time."

Silas probably did not even hear the yardman. He was already nodding his little head beneath the huge old hat before the yardman had finished speaking. He turned with a loud sniff and stamped in the direction of his office door.

The corralyard hostler, a husky man with a villainous, big, droopy dragoon mustache, rolled his eyes skyward and also went back inside the yard.

Carpenter walked his hitch for a mile before breaking it over into a loose lope. The only place he could make good time was on the Sheridan side of the mountains. Once he had the grade to contend with, he had to favor his horses. But Jack knew every blessed yard of this road all the way through the gun-sight notch and down the other side. He also knew the territory on both sides of the road for miles, even up yonder where the timber began.

He halted, as he always did, at the stone-trough turnout about seven miles above town, got the buckets to offer his horses water, and was assisted by Pepperdine, McGregor, and Reg Lee. Carpenter needed some wrinkles taken out of his bafflement, so as the four men worked he asked questions and they answered them as best they could.

When it was time to stow the buckets and leave, Jack's indignation had about reached its peak. As they were standing on the near side of the stage, he said, "I can tell you one thing: Unless they know that country up ahead, they're goin' to be a while gettin' through it. There's barrancas up in there that go arrow straight, then suddenly end in a cliff face. There's canyons they can't cross unless they sprout wings, and damned little horse feed until they're down the far side and out of the timber."

Hugh had one hand on the door latch when he asked a question. "Where would you say we'd ought to leave your stage and string out to get in front of them before they get up this far?"

Carpenter did not hesitate. "I'll show you. Get in."

118

As they were moving out, Reg observed practically that they hadn't brought food. It was beginning to look like they would not get back to town until sometime tomorrow, if then.

Pepperdine was sympathetic to the liveryman's hunger and offered his plug of molasses cured. Reg eyed the lint-encrusted little dark brown square and smiled feebly. "No thanks. Be a while before I'm that hungry."

Hugh bit off a corner under the baleful gaze of James McGregor, smiled warmly, and said, "Beats hell out of bein' hungry."

McGregor's reply was tart. "Does it now? That's a dirty habit. I heard once from a medicine peddler that it eats holes in your guts, too."

Hugh nodded pleasantly. "An' his snake oil cured that, didn't it?"

McGregor looked out the window where shadows were firming up. He had tried to chew tobacco just once and got so sick he thought he was going to die and wished to gawd he would. From that day to this he hated the stuff and, like a true-blue hypocrite, at least in this respect, never missed an opportunity to look down his nose at tobacco chewers, to scold those he knew well enough to do this to, which included his old friend the harnessmaker, and to repeat endlessly what the snake-oil peddler had told him.

Pepperdine was so accustomed to the idiosyncrasies of his old friend that he could smile through the most virulent diatribes. He was fond of McGregor. At times he wished the gunsmith had been born with a less grim outlook on life and more humor, but there was nothing anyone could do about that.

They were climbing before Reg leaned to look up

ahead. Timber created a feeling of dusk before it was that time of day, and the warmth of the open country was replaced by a very bearable and fragrant uplands coolness.

He pulled his head back in. "Should have brought blankets, too," he said. Pepperdine eyed the liveryman a trifle skeptically. "Seems to me I been on posse hunts with you other times, Reg, when you rolled up in your stinkin' saddle blanket like everyone else."

Lee remained silent for a long while, until they felt the coach slackening off and edging toward the east side of the road.

Carpenter set his binders, climbed down, yanked open the door, and turned to point. "You see that tall snag northwest maybe a mile?"

They climbed out before one of them acknowledged the existence of the tall skeleton tree. Carpenter dropped his arm. "Over there you'll find an old trail. Mostly used by animals, but I've rode over it years past on bear hunts. That's the only trail that'll meander around through the timber and take a rider all the way to the rims an' down the other side. There may be other ones like it, but they're sure as hell a lot farther west than I've hunted up through here. If them people left town keepin' the coach road in sight for their bearings, they're goin' to come on to that trail. There's other trails, mostly narrower, but they all end up in the main trail." He paused, squinting in the direction of the snag. "My guess is that they aren't up this far yet. If they are, if they got to the snag, why, then by now they'll be up ahead of you boys. I don't expect they did that, though, unless they knew this timbered country. You ought to be able to set on some high places and see their movement or their dust."

As he finished talking, Carpenter went over to the front wheel of his coach and leaned there. When McGregor asked about water up in there, the driver answered matter-of-factly, "Just about any of those deep arroyos got a trickle down in 'em."

Reg Lee had a question. "How long before you come back headin' south?"

Carpenter grinned. "Day after tomorrow, about midday." He squinted at the sun, climbed to his seat, booted off the binders, and called back just once before taking up the lines and flicking them to start the horses moving. He said, "If you find 'em an' they've harmed that lady, if you don't leave 'em hangin' up here from a tree, you don't ride back with me."

They watched him depart. McGregor sighed, looked out where the old snag leaned, and started walking. Hugh and Reg followed.

There were birds to scold them all the way to the dead tree, and a small black bear stopped them momentarily, but evidently it was an orphan, because no sow bear appeared to protect it as it fled.

There were upthrusts that they discussed using, but first they had to find the old trail. As Jack Carpenter had said, it was close to the snag. Also, it was not only wide, dusty, and well-traveled, but large animals had used it, so head clearance was just about high enough for a horseman to pass through without a lot of hunching down to avoid tree limbs.

Hugh made a guess. "Old In'ian road." They explored it up-country for a few hundred yards before returning to the snag tree. They did not explore it southward for fear of raising dust down where they hoped the outlaws would be coming up-country with their hostages.

They selected points of vantage and split up. Hugh

Pepperdine had to scramble in loose rock to get atop his little upthrust, and when he got up there, a large greenish timber rattler, not very long but almost as thick through as a man's arm, was sunning itself atop a flat rock, of which there were many on the top out.

Hugh startled the snake, which coiled and rattled at him. He picked up several rocks, tossed them, drove the viper out of its coil and down the far side of the top out.

Before settling in, Hugh used his carbine to push the other flat rocks around. At this time of year snakes were likely to be traveling in pairs. But if that one had been, Pepperdine did not find its mate.

He had an excellent view southward, but in the other three directions trees higher than his point of vantage impaired the view. He got comfortable, not altogether confident their strategy would work, even if the trail he could see was the only one to cross the mountains completely. He did not know the counterfeiters, but in his long and colorful career hell met his share of outlaws, and while he'd known some who weren't very clever, most of them had been. He assumed the ones he was watching for were.

In the middle distance, impossible to pinpoint because of the nature of the noise it made, a buck deer was rubbing his horns on a tree, occasionally butting it, and sometimes hooking the lowest limbs, then letting them snap back.

Hugh did not spend a lot of time looking for the fighting deer. He tried to imagine about how far into the mountains the renegades had gotten. He hoped their search for a trail did not end in a canyon or at the edge of a barranca, or turn eastward, perhaps as far as the stage road, and continue northward by that route.

He could not see the stage road. McGregor, who had gone in that direction when they had split up, might be able to. Hugh could not locate McGregor, even though he knew which way the gunsmith had gone.

The liveryman had angled farther up-country toward a jumble of pockmarked prehistoric rocks. They were scattered over a small area, and there were several of them tall enough to serve as a lookout. Hugh could not see him, either, although he had glimpses of the ancient boulders up through the trees.

A topknotted bluejay arrived in a nearby fir tree, saw Hugh sitting on the top out, and made enough noise to alert every creature for two hundred yards in all directions that there was a trespasser in his area.

Hugh threw seven stones before he came close enough to send the bluejay away, still scolding.

He fished around for his cut plug, got a chew settled in his cheek, tipped down his hat, and almost went to sleep. What jarred him wide awake was an old gummer bitch-wolf who appeared as a soundless wraith at the base of his vantage point, nose to the ground in her endless search for mice, baby birds, and just about anything edible excepting snakes.

He watched her for as long as her foraging continued in his area. After she disappeared westerly among the huge trees, he lost interest but was no longer drowsy.

THE SHOCK OF A LIFETIME

FOR JOE FOGARTY, WHO HAD SEEN THE STAGECOACH pass and who had viewed it indifferently, the problem of following the tracks he had found where a party of hard riders had cut a wide swath through tall grass would have been simplified if the country had not been open and practically treeless.

In order to minimize being seen on their back trail he had to stay in arroyos, where the outlaws would be unable to detect pursuit, and this was exasperating because the erosion gullies did not head straight toward the uplands, even though the gully-washing downpours that had created them had come from up there. They angled left and right. Sometimes they cut diagonally across the range before straightening out.

It was frustrating to know the outlaws with their hostages were making good time, while he dared not ride up into plain sight to do the same.

He had plenty of time to think, but at this time he was concerned only with overtaking the counterfeiters, not with reflecting on what had brought Joe Fogarty and the fugitives to this point.

He watched the sky, and as daylight waned he occasionally rode up just high enough to be able to see northward, but during none of those interludes did he see riders, and that began to worry him. It also bothered him that he could see all the way past the scrubby foothills to the timbered highlands, which meant if he left his arroyos, the people he was pursuing would be able to see just as far in reverse.

Twice he left his horse out of sight and searched for the telltale signs where the outlaws had made their wide swath through the grass. It was reassuring to know they had not changed course, but it still bothered him that he could not see them. They hadn't had all that much of a head start. At least, according to his figuring, they hadn't. Nevertheless, they were nowhere in sight.

Shadows were puddling in the deep places where he was riding, but it was much longer before they also began to mantle the open country. Fogarty tested the visibility several times, and when he could no longer see beyond the foothills, he rode up out of the low places to continue his pursuit on level country.

Of course he was taking a chance. If the counterfeiters were as coyote as most outlaws, they'd have someone hanging back expressly to watch the rearward country. Horse thieves did this, as did cattle rustlers. Counterfeiters did not quite fit in the same category with those other outlaw types, but that was nothing a man wanted to bet money on. Another thing rustlers and horse thieves were very adept at was setting up ambushes. They usually had a very good reason for doing this, especially with cattle. Horses could be run hard; cattle could not. It was the rule of those other kinds of outlaws to try to stop pursuit cold or slow it down to beat hell.

The men Marshal Fogarty was after had nothing to slow them down. They might set up a bushwhack, but he thought it unlikely, because their foremost concern was in getting out of the country as swiftly as they could.

Nevertheless, Fogarty was prudent. When he finally reached the knobby foothills, he avoided narrow places, stands of thick underbrush, and little spits of trees.

He got into the lower timbered country in about the same area where the fleeing people had reached it. From this point on he remained on their trail. There was no longer dust in the air, which meant the outlaws were far ahead.

It was gloomy among the huge trees. It was also ideal for ambushing, but he paralleled their trail from a fair distance westerly, only infrequently going over to make certain they had not changed course.

Two things puzzled him. One was the hard usage they were subjecting their stolen livestock to. No experienced riders, outlaw or otherwise, pushed saddle stock hard in mountainous country unless they wanted to end up on foot. These people had already pushed the horses hard across the open country even before reaching the security of the mountains, and they were still pushing them.

If they did not slack off soon, Marshal Fogarty was going to come on to them either leading wind-broke horses or continuing their odyssey on foot without any horses.

The other troubling factor was that he did not know these mountains very well. He'd ridden to the foothills a few times, and once or twice he'd gone a little higher, but by early evening he had already passed everything that was even vaguely familiar.

He'd heard many stories of the mountains, and one theme seemed endemic in all those tales: Unlike most parts of the Rockies, which adhered to predictable directions, this area miles north of Sheridan was like a labyrinth.

With the forest gloom deepening, Fogarty began to encounter some of the inconsistencies that made this particular area unique. He ended up at dead ends several times. In the end he abandoned caution and went over where the counterfeiters had passed along and remained on their trail, even when the growing darkness required that he dismount and lead his animal because he could not see the trail very well from the saddle.

The dusk that had settled elsewhere, down around Sheridan and across the open range country, was a more or less permanent element in the forested highlands. Even in broad daylight, because of the spiky, high treetops, only filtered sunlight reached through, and that only happened in particular areas, so Joe Fogarty had been walking ahead of his horse for more than an hour in unnatural dusk when genuine dusk had settled elsewhere. He had become accustomed to the poor light.

What he sought was the dust scent that hung in the still air of every forest. Sound could be either silenced or diffused, but the prehistoric layers of forest dust that were roiled by everything that passed through were any upland tracker's signal that he was on a live track.

The trouble was that Fogarty did not detect the dust scent until he had been walking so long his legs were beginning to ache, so he halted near a ledge of lichen rock to rest, and at this place he picked up his first hint of dust in the air.

He was encouraged by this, but because he was tired, hungry, and had been feeling slightly discouraged up to this point, his reaction was to throw a humorless grin at his horse. The animal was nosing for grass shoots in a place where grass only grew in clearings because the soil beneath the layers of needles was resin impregnated.

The horse found some dusty underbrush to pick at, but evidently the growth was bitter because it began nosing elsewhere.

Fogarty considered his tucked-up animal, and he had favored it. The animals up ahead somewhere had to be in worse condition. He speculated that the fugitives would make a camp.

When he eventually struck out again, the permanent gloom was deepening. Above the forest and around it, nightfall had arrived.

He came across a busy little narrow snow-water creek. His horse drank eagerly as Fogarty sank into the moist earth at creek side to drink, splash water over his face, and study imprints of shod hooves where the fugitives had crossed this same creek some time earlier. The water was not only cold, it was swift. There was no way of guessing how much time had passed since the fugitives had been here. The water was as clear as glass. As swiftly as it ran, it would probably cleanse itself of roiled earth within fifteen minutes of having horses plow across it.

Fogarty watched his tired animal making sideways sweeps of its head as it ravenously cropped creek-side grass. He hobbled it, slung the bridle from the horn, and with his carbine in hand crossed the creek on foot. The animal had done its best for him. It deserved consideration.

Evidently this watering place was popular. Fogarty encountered four timid does, one with spotted twins, an old gummer bitch-wolf, and several smaller animals he did not see but whose startled sounds as they fled from man scent indicated they, too, had been going to water.

The wolf might make his horse nervous, but as old and rheumatic as she appeared to be, the horse had nothing to fear, although it probably would not realize this was so.

For a hundred yards it was not difficult to follow the shodhorse sign, but after the water had been completely shaken off, Joe was back to walking bent over and upon infrequent occasions stopped to kneel and trace out the tracks with a finger.

The last time he did this he swore to himself. When were those people going to stop? They were straddling dead-tired horses. Each time Fogarty knelt to make a close inspection, the same telltale sign appeared. Tired horses made a slight dragging mark with the toe of hooves or shoes of their rear feet.

128

Fogarty had no idea of the time. He was alert, even though all the climbing and sashaying he'd done up in here had worn down his body. The reason he did not turn back and rest for a few hours beside the creek with his horse was that several times now he had picked up the distinctively musty, slightly tangy scent of disturbed fir and pine needles. He was getting closer.

An owl as large as a chicken came in from the east, passing within inches of Fogarty's face. He pulled back, and the owl, startled out of its wits by such an unlikely encounter on one of its routine sweeps of its hunting area, veered too hard to the right and slammed into a red fir, dropped to the ground, and did not move.

Fogarty stepped over, prodded the bird with his Winchester barrel until its head came around with a vicious lunge, and the powerful hooked beak locked onto the barrel. Joe raised the barrel, got the owl on its feet, shook it loose, and walked away.

He had covered about thirty yards when the muted sound of a horse clearing its nostrils came to him faintly. He stopped, leaned on his saddle gun, and tried to estimate how distant that horse had been. When he failed at this, he started forward again, suspecting that the fugitives had finally stopped for the night. The way they had been treating their animals, it probably was the darkness and the inconsistencies of the terrain more than any humane consideration of their horses that had caused them to stop.

It was harder now to see tracks, even when he sank to one knee. He moved very carefully, staying to one side of the trail. As far as he knew, the fugitives and their prisoners would be making a dry camp. If there was water up ahead somewhere, it had to be a spring or a sump, because if there had been a running creek,

Fogarty would have heard it. Now the forest and the night were utterly silent.

He had no idea where he was. There were a couple of certainties. One was that he'd covered a lot of ground before he'd dismounted to lead his horse, and also since leaving the animal at the creek. The other certainty was that he was getting close to the fugitives.

He passed several jumbles of scabrous old lava boulders, large, dull, brown-gray in color, and badly pitted. The trail had been steep but never in a direct climb, evidence that it was a very ancient pathway made by animals who never went directly up a mountainside unless being pursued or unless some obstacle such as a huge rock made climbing necessary. Otherwise, the trails angled back and forth, gaining elevation as they did so.

It had been used by large antlered animals. They had pretty well broken back limbs that would otherwise have grown across it mounted-man high.

Fogarty stopped to sniff the air. If there was a camp up ahead somewhere with people in it who were eating, their meal was cold. No smoke scent came back to him.

He followed the trail without stopping to verify the passage of shod horses. He was passing between two immense red firs when a rock up ahead rattled among other rocks. The sound and its echo were distinct. Fogarty slung the carbine into the crook of one arm before proceeding.

When he was several yards up-country from the matching fir trees, a man's voice was very distinct as he said, "All right. We got clean away, but like I been sayin', if we don't slack off an' rest these animals, we're goin' to end up on foot. Look at 'em. They're too worn down even to look for grass."

130

Fogarty continued in the direction of the voice as another man spoke. This voice was harsh and menacing. "We can't favor 'em much. By now, sure as hell they're after us. Maybe a whole posse. Maybe that damned town marshal."

The first man spoke again. His voice sounded neither harsh nor menacing; it sounded plain dog-tired. "He didn't follow us. You saw that yourself when we sat up in the trees watching back down to the open country. But hell, Cullen, even if he was comin', he'd be so far back he'd never even get close."

For a long time there was no further talking. Fogarty stepped off the trail and began sifting in among the big trees in the direction of those men who had spoken.

He did not see them, but he saw several head-hung, completely exhausted saddle horses standing together too numbed by bone weariness to even poke around for something to eat.

Fogarty eyed them briefly and wagged his head. They'd had about ten hours of hard use, no rest, no feed or water, and were not going to be treated any better tonight or tomorrow.

Fogarty finally saw the back of a couple of heads, both hatted and blending with the gloom. He crept as close as he dared and sank to one knee beside a large tree. It was impossible to see everyone up there, so he rose and sidled uphill a few yards. From this fresh point of vantage he could see down into the dry camp fairly well.

It looked like it was a whole tribe of people down there. He could not make out details very well, but he could discern each individual. There were *eight* of them.

Except for the conversation he had overheard during which one man was addressed as Cullen, he might have thought he had misread the signs somewhere and had been tracking the wrong people.

As it was, he remained stone still for a long time, puzzling over who else was there with the outlaws until he heard someone say, "Hey, beanpole, where'd you get the notion you could outflank us?"

The answering voice was too familiar to Joe Fogarty for him to be mistaken when he identified it, although the shock of finding Hugh Pepperdine a captive left him too astonished to pay attention to the harnessmaker's reply.

"I was trackin' when you was wearin' moss in your Biddies."

This time when the outlaw spoke there was an unmistakable ring of contempt. "Maybe you was, but if you was, why, then it's a darned wonder to me you lived this long, because we caught you like you was a little kid."

Hugh's retort was curt. "You never caught me. You tricked me. I saw the liveryman comin' toward me, so I got down to meet him."

"Yeah. And we was right behind him waitin' for his friends to step into sight."

"That's trickin' somebody, not trackin' them."

Fogarty sank to the ground. It wasn't just Hugh down there. The other two men with bound wrists were Reg Lee and James McGregor!

THE FEEL OF DANGER

FOGARTY WITHDREW SOUNDLESSLY, FOUND A PLACE OF concealment, and sat with his back to a big tree with the Winchester leaning against it on his right side.

How Hugh, James, and Reg Lee happened to be up

132

here was a real puzzler. He had counted those tucked-up horses. There were five, the same animals the outlaws and their hostages had used.

If the men from town had ridden up in here, they must have hidden their animals very well.

He was just as puzzled about the appearance of his old friends up here as he was at their present situation. They had not been brought up here by the outlaws, which meant they had come in pursuit of the fleeing people, but how they had been captured was something to think about. Fogarty had been on outlaw trails with at least two of them, McGregor and Pepperdine, several times. They were not greenhorns.

By the time he had recovered from his shock, the night was beginning to turn cool. He crept back, got belly-down, and inched close enough to identify Elizabeth Durning, Ernest Macy, and William Booker. It required a little more time to make out his old friends, because they were lying close to one another. The others had saddle blankets to cover themselves with. Hugh, Reg, and James did not.

He backed up a second time, made a painstaking withdrawal up and around the sleeping people to the area of the worn-out horses, got a shank on one, and began leading it southward. The other horses followed. There was no haste and no noise.

Fogarty did not free the lead horse until he had been walking it downhill for about an hour, then, as he stepped aside, he slapped the horse on the rump. It continued to follow the course of least resistance, which was down the hill. Its companions went docilely along behind it. By morning they should be out of the timber back down to the grassland.

Fogarty started back. He had accomplished the first

133

objective of any manhunter: set the prey afoot.

He rested twice. In country like this it seemed that whether a man was going or coming, it was always uphill.

By the time he was back in the area of those scabrous, old, pocked rocks, the coolness had turned into downright cold. Joe guessed he had used up about two thirds of the time left before dawn getting the saddle stock out of the country.

Someone among the people in their protected place cleared his pipes, expectorated, and made a little rattling sound as he turned and twisted his body to find his warmed place again.

Fogarty remained motionless throughout this interlude. Afterward he crept closer again, took plenty of time to locate Macy and Booker, who would be armed, and began approaching them very quietly from the rear.

They were lying about fifteen feet apart, coats buttoned to their throats, hats pulled down to their ears, bodies huddled beneath the amply long but not quite wide enough smelly saddle blankets.

He raised up above them beside a huge, overripe fir tree, taking plenty of time to make his capture with as little risk as possible. He did not think he would get a second chance if he botched the first one.

It was already botched.

Someone across the way raised his head, like a turtle, turned it slowly, and remained like that for a time, then sank back down. Joe guessed that had been either James or Hugh.

Across interminable distance, coming from a greater elevation, otherwise the sound probably would not have carried so far, the scream of a big cat made the back

134

hairs of every creature that heard it stand straight up.

Fogarty was reaching for his hip holster and froze for several seconds. There was no immediate danger and he knew it. There probably would have been no danger even if the mountain lion had been close enough to see or scent him, but that unnerving scream at any time, even in broad daylight, could and usually did stop all movement, scatter every thought, and strike unreasoning fear into the heart of every creature who heard it.

Fogarty's right hand was on the saw-handle grip of his belt gun and remained there as he very slowly turned his head to see if the cougar's cry had awakened anyone. The difficult-to-discern lumps were as they had been. If anyone down there had heard the cry, he was remaining perfectly still.

Fogarty waited. If it required ten or fifteen minutes for the exhausted people to go back to sleep, he would wait. There could be no error when he finally crept down between Macy and Booker to awaken them with a cold gun barrel.

The silence stretched out, deepened as time passed without even nocturnal critters rustling needles or making their little garrulous sounds.

Fogarty straightened up to advance, and a round, hard object was pressed into his back over the kidneys unaccompanied by any sound. He stopped breathing for seconds as he leaned away from the pressure. It followed him. He started to twist from the waist. A threatening voice said, "Drop the gun . . . I said—*drop it!*"

He recognized the voice even in its unnatural tone. The man he had come to believe would be the most dangerous of the fugitives was behind him. Cullen Dowd.

He dropped the six-gun.

Gun pressure did not slacken. "Face forward!"

Fogarty obeyed.

The burly, bearded man's voice turned bitter. "I knew it. I warned them. I told the damned fools. You got a belly gun or a boot knife?"

"No."

"If you're lyin', Marshal, I'm goin' to—"

"I don't carry hideout weapons. Never have."

Dowd's tone changed slightly. "Walk down there, take your time, an' keep both arms away from your sides. *Move!*"

Fogarty moved. He only had about twenty feet to traverse to be in the center of the camp. When he was told to halt, he did so. Up to this moment he had not seen his captor, but as the freighter aimed a kick at someone's boot soles, Fogarty caught a full-length view of him. He also acted on the instinct that told him that unless he believed in miracles, he was not going to leave this place alive.

He did little more than shift his weight, not enough movement in forest darkness to be detected by someone who was not looking at him, and kicked out viciously. The blow caught Cullen Dowd on the upper left leg. Its force sent him falling across one of the sleeping lumps. He tried to twist and raise his gun arm, but Fogarty, whose size and power were those of an individual who would not normally be expected to be fast, went after him with a desperation caused by a conviction that the husky, bearded man was the deadliest of his enemies.

The man Dowd had fallen on let go with an outward burst of breath followed, by a loud squawk as he fought to get out from beneath the weight of the freighter. When Fogarty landed atop the freighter, the man being

136

crushed beneath them made strangling sounds and lashed out with both arms and both legs.

Fogarty missed his lunge at Dowd's gun arm but blocked it when the freighter tried frantically to hoist his arm high enough to turn the gun inward to fire it. Fogarty's second lunge at the burly man's arm was successful. His fingers closed around Dowd's wrist like steel coils. He used Dowd's own straining effort to lever himself backward enough to aim a fist. Dowd saw it coming and rolled his head. The blow struck flesh and bone. The man they had fallen upon turned loose all over.

Dowd tried bringing up a crippling knee. Fogarty twisted enough to take the force of the knee on his hip. He had to lower his head almost to the freighter's chest to avoid a flying fist, but Dowd was not left-handed, so his aim was bad. Joe pushed half-upright, threw a punch, and this time the sound of a granite fist sliding upward over jawbone, cheekbone, and all the way to the temple of the bearded man was similar to the noise made by a blanket tearing. Dowd's reflexes were so badly impaired that although he was still conscious and willing to fight, his left fist not only lacked power, it did not connect.

Fogarty bored in. He aimed from the shoulder, and when his fist landed, Cullen Dowd went limp all over. Fogarty wrenched the six-gun from him, kicked free of both men, and sprang upright. On his left a sleeper was sitting straight up fumbling among pine needles on his opposite side where he'd rolled his shell-belt with the holster on top.

Fogarty stepped over, brought the handgun down, but the other man was already rolling as rapidly as possible to his right.

Fogarty broke it off, raced for the timber, and did not halt until his heart sounded as though it might break loose in its dark place.

The weapon in his fist was one of those Lightning Colts. He would have traded a very good horse right at this moment for the gun he'd abandoned back there where Dowd had crept up behind him.

There was pandemonium back in the camp. Macy and Booker were shouting threats at their captives. Fogarty leaned against a tree sucking air. It only occurred to him when it was too late that if he had gone back at the height of the chaos he probably could have either captured or shot both the other fugitives.

The distant noise lessened. Fogarty rested for a long time. It was not just the battle that had exhausted him; it was the culmination of sleeplessness, exhaustive physical effort over the past twenty-four hours, and diminishing physical reserves resulting from not having eaten in a long while.

He crawled into a thicket of skunk brush where the ferns reached two feet overhead and did not move until he heard birds making their drowsy dawn sounds.

He did not sleep, but he did not move, either, not until the cold was beginning to lessen and the upland gloom had begun to acquire some of the strange, cathedrallike opaqueness that was its normal day-long light.

He recovered slowly. He had escaped by the narrowest of margins. More to the point, even though Dowd would recover and be more deadly than ever, Fogarty had set them all on foot, and that would give him another opportunity, providing he was patient and careful.

When he was ready to leave the skunk brush, its smell was imbedded in his clothing. That might mean something to wild animals, but it would be detectable to two-legged critters only if he was close to them.

With the heat beginning to penetrate, Fogarty slipped westerly until he could see the camp from among tall trees. It was empty. He had not expected it to be otherwise. There was only one horse left, the animal he had left back by the little brawling creek. He did not expect the fugitives to go back in that direction, but as he began moving northward, he watched for any indication that they might have.

The signs he found made him scowl. He had assumed they would continue up-country. It had been obvious yesterday that their purpose was to cross the rims and go down the far slopes northward.

Evidently they'd decided that doing this now, with at least one lawman pressing them, would probably result in their eventual capture, since anyone pursuing them would be on horseback.

The tracks led in the opposite direction. Southward, back down in the direction from which they had ridden the day before, and that didn't make any sense to Joe Fogarty. By now the whole countryside down around Sheridan would know something was happening. There would be inquisitive riders out. Sheridan had a very good coterie of town possemen. The men were mostly seasoned, experienced, and willing.

Macy, Booker, and Dowd probably did not know this, otherwise, it seemed to Joe Fogarty, they would be traveling in any direction but back the way they had come.

But a mile farther along Fogarty got another surprise.

The tracks of all those walking people very abruptly turned eastward.

There was a possibility that they would find his horse,

even though they were farther south than the crossing where he had left the animal, but it was an unacceptable risk. Joe Fogarty had no intention of also being set afoot, so he abandoned the trail and struck out over the shortest route to the creek crossing. He had left two good guns back there.

He made fairly good time. He did not have to slant uphill very much, and with such daylight as there was in this place visibility was good enough. He had become so adjusted to it that he did not even miss brighter light.

The horse was standing hipshot not very far north along the creek where Fogarty had left it. It was dozing in one of the shafts of sunlight that penetrated the treetops. Until Fogarty appeared, the horse was perfectly comfortable and entirely at peace. It eyed the approaching man with no warmth at all, even though they had been together for several years.

Fogarty used his hobbles as a shank and led the horse back to where his outfit was. He used a half-breed latigo and had to set the buckle tongue down three holes from where he usually put it. There was no doubt that the horse had slept, but it had also done something else to a greater length; it had grazed off all the creek-side grass for a fair distance up and down the creek.

Fogarty swung up and reined down-country to locate the fugitives' sign again. He did not feel entirely confident they would still be traveling eastward, but they were. He found a place where they had stopped briefly at the brawling creek. From this point on he rode slowly and stopped often to listen. He did not believe they could be very far ahead.

He not only hung back to allow them plenty of time to stay ahead, he also moved along very cautiously. Cullen Dowd had the best reason in the world for trying to catch the Sheridan town marshal tracking the people he was with.

VERY, VERY CLOSE

WHEN IT WAS CLEAR THE TRACKS GOING EASTWARD were not likely to alter course, Fogarty angled away from them farther up the slope. He knew as well as he knew his name that there was a man down there waiting to kill him.

Heat arrived slowly. It was a blessing to someone who had been uncomfortably chilly along toward the tag end of the previous night. It also encouraged drowsiness in a man who had been without sleep for more than twenty-four hours. But the horse never faltered. The only outward manifestation of its rest beside the creek was that it sweated copiously, as all horses did after filling up on watery feed.

After a couple of hours of hearing nothing, Fogarty was tempted to drop back down closer to the fugitives' trail. He did not yield to this for another hour, when he was beginning to feel uneasy. If the fugitives and their prisoners had changed course again, Fogarty could have been riding farther from them as time passed.

He left the horse hobbled again and passed among big trees on the down slope until he picked up the scent of ancient dust. From this point on he was even more careful. He used up a half hour gliding Indian-like from tree to tree in order to get close enough to see the tracks left by the walking people.

By the time he got that close the sun was directly overhead, its rays being spread fanlike over treetops and penetrating in only a few places. In those places it was not necessary to smell the dust. It made a faintly shimmering veil across each sunbeam.

The fugitives were still traveling eastward.

On his way back uphill, it occurred to Fogarty that what those outlaws might have in mind was reaching the stage road. Their reason for doing this would be to wait until either horsemen or someone driving a buggy or a wagon passed along. If they caught someone with a wagon they could make better time than by walking, but if they could catch several mounted people, they could do even better. With horses under them again their chances of escaping would improve vastly.

Fogarty looped his hobbles behind the cantle, snugged up the cinch, and struck out straight eastward. Whether his conjecture was correct or not, the people he was tracking were going to come into sight of the roadway before too long.

He picked up the gait a little, made no further attempts to locate them, and continued to ride until he came across a long-spending thin ridge and could see out through the trees and sunshine in the narrow, long cut where the road showed as a grayish ribbon two wagons wide and nearly as straight as an arrow.

He went down toward it by veering in and out among the trees. Where he halted, the road was below him about a hundred and fifty feet, which would have been an acceptable distance if he'd had his Winchester.

All he had was that little Lightning Colt, and while there were certainly instances where a double-action revolver had an advantage over regulation single-action handguns, this was not one of them. What he needed was something with better accuracy and greater range.

He inched ahead a few yards at a time. He thought he was ahead of the people on foot. There was no sign of

142

them. But most towns had graveyards with people eternally resting in them who had guessed wrong in situations like this.

Huge trees stood in thick tiers all the way down to the side of the roadway on both sides. Fogarty sighed aloud and dismounted to leave the horse hobbled again. A man on a horse made an excellent target. He did not cherish the idea of going down to the edge of the road, but mostly he did not like the idea of having to climb back up the damned hill to his horse.

If he ever quit his job as marshal in Sheridan and went somewhere else to seek similar employment, it was going to be in flat country as sure as gawd had made little green apples.

He could not avoid raising dust as he went down the slope, more dust, in fact, than his horse should have raised. But there wasn't much he could do about that except to halt occasionally to scan the area and to hope very hard that the people he was after would have seen the road by now and would not be interested in anything else.

He was two thirds of the way down when a five-point buck sprang out of a shady bed, thumped the ground hard, and bounded up the hill as though his life depended upon it, which it might have at another time.

That made more dust.

Fogarty was turning away from the big deer when the sound of a wheeled vehicle came to him from the north. It was faint but unmistakable.

He went down the last hundred feet in a sliding hurry. If the people on foot were close enough to have heard that rig coming, they would also hasten to the edge of the road.

On Fogarty's part it was unnecessary anxiety. When

143

the vehicle finally appeared, coasting easily on the downgrade, it was a stripped-down wagon bed with huge wheels, probably taken from a freight wagon, with three brawny men sitting up there amid steel tools. Behind them was a load of green fir logs. Their horses were eighteen-hundred pounders with feathered fetlocks, thick manes and foretops, and Roman noses.

Even without the logs and the men, that wagon and its great horses would not be something anyone in flight would choose to make haste with.

The men were talking and passing a burlap-wrapped gallon jug back and forth as they shook and tattled. The big, old running gear was without springs. By the time it had come up and passed on by, there was a dust banner fifteen feet high in its wake.

Fogarty got into tree shade, set his back to a forest mammoth, and tipped down his hat to watch the only moving thing in sight. He guessed that somewhere south of him Booker, Macy, and Cullen Dowd were doing the same thing. Perhaps even thinking the same thought. Fogarty would have given a month's pay for a turn at that jug.

The dust was settling when a frail, little top buggy with tassels and two elderly men came up-country from the direction of Sheridan. Fogarty made his appraisal of this outfit, too, and discarded it as something the outlaws would make a run at. For one thing, it had one seat, wide enough for two passengers, and no wider. It had a little "box" behind the seat, large enough for a picnic hamper and very little else. But most discouraging for the fugitives was the animal pulling the rig. It was a mare, gray at the muzzle and over the eyes, with a perfectly flat chin and sunken places above each eye. She was in fair shape, considering that she had probably shed at least half of her grinders as she progressed toward perhaps about twenty years of age.

Fogarty tried to hear what the old men were discussing but caught only a couple of words. One was "Antietam" and the other one was a compound word: "Damnsecesh."

Fogarty's drowsiness returned. Heat in the slot made shimmery waves up the roadway. Deer flies appeared. They kept him awake. When one of those things landed on a man and bit, the sting was almost as bad as that of a bee.

From the north there was the steady sound of riders moving along at a fair clip. Fogarty forgot the drowsiness, even the deer flies. He straightened up off his tree and leaned to look up-country.

By now the fugitives and their prisoners would certainly be somewhere south of him, also hiding and watching. Fogarty had a dry throat. He alternately looked up the road for a sighting of the riders and examined the Lightning Colt he'd acquired from Cullen Dowd. Its parrot-beak handle did not fit his hand well. The gun was too light. But worst of all, if there was a fight, he had belt loops with forty-five-caliber bullets in them, and the gun in his hand was forty-one caliber.

If there was a fight, it was going to have to be fought pretty much by the oncoming horsemen. Then he saw them and his breath ran out very slowly.

It was a company of cavalrymen. There was an officer out front and beside him was a red-faced, fleshy sergeant old enough to be his father. There were thirty of them, all well mounted on big bay horses.

Fogarty snickered to himself and did not move until they had passed along. Then, certain the fugitives would be watching them with covetous eyes, he turned southward and made his way for about a hundred yards before finding another big tree to shelter him.

He did not see anyone, but he knew they were down there, because as the troopers passed southward someone made a thin, angry high curse.

The sun moved, slanting to Fogarty's side of the road and farther, kept moving until the highest rims appeared to have a reddening effect upon it. But even as shadows began filling the slot where the road was, very faintly, like a diluted tan mist, Fogarty heard what was unmistakably a stagecoach. It was coming up-country, probably from Silas Browning's corralyard. This was something the fugitives might try to capture. Silas always put six horses on the pole of his northbound rigs because they had to haul their outfit up through the mountains.

Six horses would not be enough, but six horses would be better than no horses. If Booker, Macy, and Cullen still had Hugh, James, and Reg with them, as well as the deputy U.S. marshal and the Pinkerton lady, they would require eight horses.

Fogarty speculated about who they would leave behind. Probably two of his friends, either Hugh and James, or Reg Lee.

But Fogarty did not speculate for very long. Whether the outlaws suspected it or not—and at least the freighter might—not many harness horses were also broken to ride. As far as Fogarty knew, old Silas did not buy "combination" horses. They were usually too expensive for someone who did not need horses broken to pull *and* to ride. Old Silas never parted with a copper penny if he could avoid doing so. Neither did most other folks.

The stage had a long trail of dust in its wake. The

driver had been pushing his horses. But he dropped them back to a steady walk long before he felt the land tilting through the seat of his britches.

Fogarty leaned out trying to identify the driver. He thought it might be Jack Carpenter. He had no way of knowing it would not be, but three other watchers hidden among the trees southward knew it wouldn't be. Jack had told Hugh, James, and Reg that he would not be returning southward until tomorrow.

The horses were lightly sweating as they entered the slot. They were "warmed out" for the long northward pull. They would not have to lean against their collar pads for a mile or so yet, but they were prepared to do it.

There were two men on the high seat. One was a middlesized man Fogarty did not recognize. He had a Winchester rifle instead of a carbine between his knees. Beside him was Browning's corralyard boss, a large, gruff, rough man. He only drove when no one else was available.

Fogarty tried to see if there were passengers. If there were, they were keeping their heads inside.

The coach came steadily ahead. When it passed from sunlight into that canyon-tan wall of late-day shadow, Fogarty stood up. By now the fugitives would be exasperated enough at the delay to be willing to settle for a stagecoach. At least it had room for all of them. They might have figured by now that the more hostages they had, the better their bargaining position if they were eventually run to ground.

But whatever they had thought or discussed, the stagecoach was very likely to be their last opportunity to acquire something that would get them out of the country. With darkness on the way, their chances of escaping northward were even better. For as long as daylight remained, people who saw stagecoaches paid them little attention. Stagecoaches had a legitimate reason for being on the road. Even Fogarty had to admit to himself that while he'd known of dozens of stagecoaches to be stopped and robbed, he had never heard of one being taken over and used by outlaws in an attempt to get out of the country.

With unseen eyes riveted on it, the stage suddenly stopped a half mile southward. The gruff driver handed his lines to the gun guard and climbed irritably to the ground. He walked ahead, placed his right hand on the rump of a wheeler, and ran his left hand down the animal's leg so it would know he was there and what he was doing, which it would not otherwise have known because it was fitted with blinders. With a grunt he lifted the leg, yanked a tug to the outside, let the foot back down, and looked up at the gun guard as he said, "Two links farther out than the other tug."

The gun guard answered without changing expression. "It's goin' to happen as long as Silas hires anyone he can get dirt cheap."

The driver swung up the side, paused on the wheel hub to say something reassuring to a man whose face appeared out the window, then climbed the rest of the way.

He took back the lines, sprayed amber to his left, and talked up the hitch. As the horses leaned into their collars, Fogarty was sure he had seen movement among the trees on the west side of the road about five wagon-lengths from where he was being camouflaged by tree-trunk and predusk shadows.

Fogarty scarcely breathed as the stagecoach ground ahead behind lightly straining horses. The whip and gun

148

guard were talking, but none of what they said was distinguishable to Fogarty, who was beginning to stiffen as he ignored the vehicle to concentrate on the shadowy place where he seen vague and indistinct movement.

He thought he was within Lightning Colt range, but he'd never had one of those little guns before. Whether he was or not, he felt seriously deprived by not having his own single-action forty-five.

In order to minimize the danger of not being close enough, he started moving very carefully southward. When the stagecoach was less than a hundred and fifty yards distant, he began looking for a place of concealment. He settled for a manzanita thicket and squatted down to wait. He was less than a hundred feet from the road, slightly above it. Unless those outlaws had moved, they were about three times that distance south of him on the same side of the road.

"DROP IT!"

THE STAGECOACH WAS APPROACHING THE GENERAL area where Fogarty thought the attack would take place when traffic from the north echoed down the canyon. He grudgingly took his gaze off the stagecoach to look in that direction.

Because of a slight rise in the roadway, although sound traveled well enough, the vehicles and travelers who made it were not visible for several minutes after their noise had preceded them. Fogarty had noticed this before. First with the woodcutters and again with the cavalrymen.

He noticed it now as the sounds increased without anything being in sight to indicate what had made them.

149

He shot a quick look southward. If the stage driver had heard anything, he gave no sign of it, but then between his desultory conversation with the gun guard and the racket his own outfit was making, he probably wouldn't have.

Of the people hidden between Fogarty and the stagecoach, there was no sign. He could imagine their exasperation. Right up until the moment when the northward travelers had telegraphed their presence ahead of them from the echo-carrying canyon walls, Macy, Dowd, and Booker had probably been as coiled and ready as striking snakes.

Fogarty heard someone call out as a party of horsemen saw the stagecoach. The foremost rider threw up his right arm, palm forward. The coach driver grudgingly pulled his horses slightly to the right. If the road had not been excavated to a depth of about fifteen feet, he would not have left the center of the road; he'd have let the riders break out around him on both sides. It was easier for them to maneuver than it was for him. However, he could not do this now because there was not enough clearance on either side, so he edged easterly as far as he could and stopped to allow the horsemen to pass. It hadn't been necessary for him to stop. The horsemen could have strung out on his near side, but since he did stop, they came alongside on his left.

There were four of them. Two were leading a pair of big brown mules. Every one of the four men looked like he'd been sleeping in his clothes for a long time and had been nowhere near a pair of shears or a razor since early last spring. But they were good-natured when their leader leaned on his oversized saddle horn and asked Silas's driver how much farther it might be down to Sheridan.

When the driver replied, the horseman nodded his thanks and held an arm toward the man nearest him, who unslung a canteen and passed it over. The horsemen were grinning as their spokesman handed the canteen up to the driver. "Green River gold," the horseman said, and laughed.

The driver sniffed, tilted the canteen, swallowed a couple of times, and handed the canteen to the gun guard. When the container was being passed back to the horseman, he addressed the driver. "Mister, we're real obliged to you for your road courtesy. Ain't all whips would do that much for mounted men."

A gaunt, elderly man alighted from the coach and walked forward to eye the raffish-looking riders. He scowled up at the driver. "You goin' to keep to your schedule, mister?" he snapped, marched back, climbed in, and slammed the door.

The horsemen were still smiling as they watched the older man depart. Their spokesman raised a hand to his hat brim and reined away.

While Joe Fogarty had been watching and listening, he had also been trying to anticipate what was going to happen next. If he had been in the boots of the outlaws hiding on the west edge of the road, he would let the stagecoach pass and make a run on the mounted men. They had four ridable horses. The mules were probably not broke to ride.

What complicated things was that the riders were already moving southward before the stagecoach got angled back to the center of the road on its northward course.

The riders were leaving the immediate area while the stagecoach was only just beginning to. If Macy and his partners jumped the mounted men, the whip, the gun

151

guard, and that old man inside the coach would see this happen. And they would be behind the outlaws, who would be facing away from them to challenge the horsemen.

Fogarty waited. For the fugitives watching those four saddle animals leaving their immediate area, the strain must have been terrible. He was beginning to believe they were not going to do anything, when sudden movement on his right brought him fully around.

Elizabeth Durning half slid, half tumbled from the slightly elevated height where the outlaws were in concealment, fell to all fours in the road, and cried out.

Her hair was awry, her dress was stained and torn in several places, and as she got to her feet with those four riders staring back at her, she beat roadway dust off her skirt.

Fogarty was motionless.

The horsemen turned back, expressionless and clearly dumbfounded by the sight of a woman standing where there had not been a living soul when they and the stage driver had briefly visited only minutes before.

Fogarty got over his astonishment as the riders started back. He stood up very slowly, pushed through his thorny cover, and from behind it began figuring passage among the large trees southward. Whatever happened out in the roadway, with everyone's attention on the little drama being enacted out there, this would be his best—probably his only—chance to get behind the outlaws.

The same unkempt individual, with little pale eyes nearly hidden when he smiled, who had spoken to the stage driver drew rein a few feet from Elizabeth Durning, leaned down on his big saddle horn, and made a drawling statement. "Lady, you hadn't ought to be

152

scourin' around up in them mountains by yourself. What happened to your horse?"

That was all he was able to say before someone out of sight to his left, up among the forest gloom where large trees were closely spaced, cocked a gun.

The riders turned slowly, ranging searching stares up the hill. Their spokesman was no longer smiling. The silence ran on. A horse stamped at harassing deer flies, but that was the only sound until a man spoke.

"Shuck your weapons an' set real still."

Fogarty placed the voice. It came from behind one of several trees slightly ahead of him and to his right. He palmed the Lightning Colt without making a sound.

The shaggy-headed rider was still leaning on his saddle horn when he said, "Mister, if it's money you want, we ain't got any. An' we won't have any until we get down yonder and sell these mules." The spokesman spoke in a quiet drawl. From what Fogarty could see of him, the man did not appear the least bit frightened.

This time when the hidden outlaw spoke, there was an unmistakable edge to his voice. "Drop the guns. I don't make a habit of repeatin' myself."

The shaggy-headed man sighed, slowly straightened in the saddle, looked around at his companions, and shrugged. When he dropped his six-gun to the roadway, his companions did the same. Then the spokesman slowly raised his left hand to tip his hat down a little as he addressed Elizabeth Durning. "Lady, if your partner's got some notion of stealin' our animals, he's goin' to be in a peck of trouble. An' you'll be right out here in the middle of it."

Fogarty ignored this exchange. He had figured out which tree was hiding the outlaw who had spoken. He was also almost certain the speaker had been Cullen Dowd. He switched the Lightning Colt to his left hand, wiped sweat off his right palm on his pants leg, and shifted the weapon back to his dry hand. As he was doing this, another voice spoke from hiding, this time from almost directly in front of Fogarty but about fifty or sixty feet closer to the edge of the bluff above the road.

"Get down. Stay on the right side of your horses. Slow now. Real slow. Dismount!"

The men did exactly as they had been ordered. Fogarty's gun hand was sweaty again. He began to ease downward very slowly. The fugitive who had spoken this time had been Ernest Macy. He and Joe Fogarty had spoken often enough for the lawman to make a positive identification.

What happened next stopped Joe Fogarty cold. Hugh Pepperdine walked to the edge of the barranca with a six-gun dangling in his big fist at his right side. He stood up there looking down at the four men who were staring up at him. Then he slid down to the roadway, ignored the light tan dirt on his britches, and went among the saddled animals lifting out Winchesters and pitching them toward the opposite side of the road.

Joe Fogarty was transfixed. He could not believe what he was seeing.

When Pepperdine was finished, he looked up the hill from where Cullen Dowd gave him an order. "Search 'em for hideouts. If you find one, be real careful. You understand?"

Hugh nodded and moved toward the stationary horsemen. Fogarty thought he saw Hugh's lips move sightly as he was searching the pale-eyed man, but that could have been an illusion. The light was poor. When Hugh stepped back, looking upward, he said, "Clean as a whistle. Not even a boot knife."

154

There was a long interval of silence during which the very brief, wind-born echo of a distant stagecoach came down the canyon from the north.

Ernest Macy called to Cullen Dowd, "Let's go." As he said this, Macy stepped from behind a tree and straightened up to his full height. Joe Fogarty let out a long breath and began raising the Lightning Colt. At that distance he could not have missed if he'd been using a slingshot.

Dowd was slow in responding. He did not seem anxious to step away from his hiding place. William Booker rose on Fogarty's right, at about the same elevation. He was holding a saddle gun in both hands. Fogarty could see his profile clearly enough to see tensed jaw muscles.

Macy spoke again. "Cullen, we don't have forever. If that damned marshal beat it back to Sheridan for a posse, they're damned likely to be on their way up here. Let's go!"

Cullen finally glided into Fogarty's sight. He had one six-gun in his holster, another one in his front waistband, and was holding a carbine in both hands. He gestured with it for the men in the roadway to walk away from their horses.

That shaggy-headed man with the pale eyes shook his head at Cullen. "Mister, you could have done better. None of our horses is shod. They been gettin' tender since yestiddy. We figured to sell the mules for money to get 'em shod with, then maybe buy a couple of younger animals and keep goin' south. You gents push these horses and you'll be lucky if you get ten miles."

Cullen moved to the edge of the barranca. When he did this, Macy and Booker also started forward. Fogarty spared a moment to look at Elizabeth Durning. With

155

dusk on the way, it was not possible to see how white her face was, but there were other indications that she was frozen in place.

Cullen glanced over his shoulder before looking down to where he would have to slide to reach the roadway. Fogarty's heart stood still, but evidently the bearded freighter had not seen him, because he faced forward and, with everyone watching, tested the crumbly earth with his Winchester butt, eased down, and made his sliding descent.

Fogarty ground his teeth. Dowd had two of those riders directly behind him. Macy and Booker also got down the little crumbly slope.

Two things had prevented Fogarty from starting the fight earlier. One was Hugh Pepperdine being down among the horsemen, and the other one was Elizabeth Durning. She would be hit the moment the fight started. She would be, as that pale-eyed man had said, in the middle of anything that happened.

She still was. So was Hugh.

Fogarty's turn had come. His mouth was as dry as cotton. His gun palm was slippery again. Sweat ran beneath his shirt. He stared straight at Cullen Dowd, and was simultaneously raising his gun and parting his lips to speak when a growly, harsh voice spoke from farther back up the slope where James McGregor had witnessed everything.

"Macy! You said you'd turn us loose!"

The answer from the roadway was curt. "Chew your way out, you old goat." Macy was reaching for a pair of reins as he said this. Dowd and Booker also started to mount. McGregor called again. "You're goin' to get yourself killed, Macy."

This time no one answered.

156

Fogarty's moment had come. With the three outlaws sitting atop horses, there was less chance of him hitting Hugh, the Pinkerton lady, or any of those four unkempt horsemen who had retreated past the center of the road toward the eastern side.

He had been more than twenty-four hours getting to this precise moment. He could not have taken the risk ten minutes earlier, and unless he took it now, he very likely would never take it at all.

He did not have to cock the Lightning Colt. All he had to do was aim and pull the trigger. He raised the gun and called to the men in the roadway.

"Don't move. If you do, it'll be like shootin' crows off a fence."

Macy, Dowd, and Booker swung in their saddles to stare up the hill. Fogarty took two steps to the right to be in plain sight.

The only movement for three or four seconds was when Elizabeth Durning clasped both hands tightly over her stomach. Fogarty said, "Hugh, drop that gun."

Pepperdine dropped it, but he also spoke. "It's not loaded. They emptied it when they told me to come down here and go over those fellers."

Fogarty aimed directly at Cullen Dowd's chest. "Drop it! The one in your britches first, then the one in your holster." When Dowd did not move, Fogarty's finger inside the trigger guard tightened. "You're one breath away from gettin' killed."

Dowd's tongue flicked over chapped lips with the speed of a snake's tongue. William Booker suddenly whined at Dowd, "Do it, for crissake, Cullen. All hell's going to bust loose if you don't."

All hell broke loose, anyway.

157

GUNS AND MEN

IT WASN'T CULLEN DOWD WHO PRECIPITATED THE VERY brief but very violent battle; it was that shockle-headed, pale-eyed man Hugh had whispered to when he had searched him for a hideout weapon.

From a distance of about forty feet, and without a challenge or a word of warning, he shot William Booker off his horse. It was doubtful that Booker knew what hit him. All the animals were badly frightened by the sudden and unexpected muzzle blast.

The mules broke free and went southward in their peculiar peg-leg lope. Dowd and Macy had their weapons up, but their frightened mounts were barely controllable and continually cakewalked, fought the bits, and swapped ends. Even so, Cullen Dowd got off a shot up the slope. It missed by two yards. Fogarty tried tracking the outlaw. Every time he began to squeeze the trigger, Dowd's panicky horse would violently move.

Hugh Pepperdine grabbed the Pinkerton lady's arm and unceremoniously dragged her to the east side of the road where the only one of those four mule owners who had a weapon was ignoring everything as he tried his damnedest to get a decent aim at Ernest Macy.

From back up among the trees James McGregor had seen Joe Fogarty step into plain sight and was yelling at him now. "Shoot! Shoot, dammit. *Shoot!*"

Cullen got his mount broadside to the bluff and fired first. He fired three times, as fast as he could tug the trigger of his Lightning Colt. He should have hit Fogarty. He most likely would have but for the fact that shooting off the hurricane deck of a terrified horse is the worst place a man can be when he's trying to use a gun accurately.

Fogarty did not flinch when a bullet flattened against the tree nearest him. He was concentrating on anticipating the frenzied horse's movement. After Cullen fired, his mount bogged its head, but Dowd had the beast on a short rein. If it could not buck its rider off, it could possibly run with him. The horse flung up its head to get the bit behind its bridle teeth on both sides and in front of its grinders. It could then lock both upper and lower teeth together, neutralize the bit, and run for it.

While its head was up, the animal was momentarily still. That was when Joe Fogarty fired off one round. He could have kept right on squeezing the trigger, but he was accustomed to single-action firing when a man had a moment to see where his slug had gone before cocking up the next round.

Dowd sat straight up in his saddle, but he was twisting to fire back. There was no sign that he had been hit, and Fogarty was preparing to try again when Ernest Macy dropped low as that pale-eyed freighter fired at him. Macy twisted his head half around, saw his adversary hauling back for another shot, and fired at the pale-eyed man while still holding his weapon sideways in his lap.

It was close enough. The horseman's old hat rose abruptly into the air and sailed sideways about fifteen feet before tumbling to the ground with about as much grace as a gut-shot bird.

The horseman's shot went wild. His friends, who were behind him, scattered like autumn leaves. The pale-eyed man knew another bullet was coming. Macy was still glaring at him with bared teeth. The horseman

159

threw himself sideways, fell, and rolled. Macy did indeed fire, but this time he missed by a far wider margin. He was still crouching over, handgun held somewhere in his lap near the seating leather, when Hugh Pepperdine came up over the rump of his horse, frightening the animal so badly that it tucked up its rear end and tried to catapult ahead. The result was that the horse fell hard with old Pepperdine gripping a handful of Macy's hair. Macy's leg was pinned, but briefly. The moment he lost the reins, the horse could use its head and neck to lever itself into a rising position. It sprang up and bolted in blind terror.

It struck Cullen Dowd's animal on the near side, almost knocking the horse to its knees, and certainly slamming Dowd forward against the Texas A-fork so hard he could barely push back. He still gripped the six-gun, and he was still obsessed with killing Joe Fogarty, who had moved but was still in plain sight up the barranca.

Dowd could not control the horse. He swung his right leg over and came down on both feet in the center of the road. Now he could be accurate. Now, too, he was a stationary target. Fogarty fired twice and watched the burly, bearded man instinctively brace one leg slightly behind the other one and raise his left hand to help steady the sixgun.

Fogarty fired one more shot.

Dowd's aimed gun hung motionless for seconds. The finger inside the trigger guard was still curled but without sufficient strength to constrict.

Dowd went down like a tree, without making any attempt to break the fall. Dust flew, his weapon lazily spun in a half circle, and someone yelled—not at Marshal Fogarty but at Hugh Pepperdine, who was

160

pummeling Ernest Macy with a rawboned, old scarred fist. The shouting was coming from behind Fogarty and to his left somewhere in the forest gloom, where an agitated gunsmith had been straining so hard to break free of his bindings that both wrists were raw.

"That's enough, Hugh! What the hell are you tryin' to do? He's unconscious, for crissake!"

Two of those shaggy-headed horsemen came up to the harnessmaker, one on each side, grabbed him, and carried him backward with rough force.

Fogarty slid down the slope, landed on his feet, and approached Cullen Dowd. He leaned for a moment, then toed Dowd faceup. Dowd had been hit four times, which meant that Joe's first shot, the one he had fired while Dowd had been in his saddle, had hit the man.

He leaned lower, considered the location of the wounds, straightened back, looked down at the double-action weapon in his fist, and threw it away.

One forty-five slug at that distance would have knocked Dowd out of his saddle. One more would have killed him. Four forty-one slugs had made a sieve out of him.

McGregor was squawking again. This time he was joined by Reg Lee. Pepperdine shook off the horsemen and started toward the crumbly slope. As he passed Marshal Fogarty he tossed something at his feet and spoke without looking away from the distant trees. "That's your gun. Dowd got it where you dropped it back up yonder."

The gun was empty, so Fogarty stood out there ignoring the voices and the movement, plugging loads into the cylinder. When he dropped the old weapon into his holster, he felt as though he were fully dressed again.

Two of those horsemen were administering to Ernest Macy. Evidently Pepperdine's mood when he had vaulted up over the horse's rump was murderous. Probably with justification. Macy and his companions had been making life miserable for the three merchants from Sheridan since capturing them.

Fogarty saw the Pinkerton lady sitting over near the eastside slope and strolled over there. He looked like the wrath of God and felt like it as he nodded and sank down near her.

She had dark rings under her eyes. Her short curly hair showed disarray, but nowhere nearly as much as it might have if she'd had long hair. Her dress was stained and torn. She sat like a mummy, looking out where the carnage had taken place while clasping both hands between her knees. She did not seem aware of Joe Fogarty's presence, but evidently she was, because she spoke in a strained voice.

"It wasn't necessary, Marshal. Booker was a weak man. He wanted to give up. Macy and Cullen Dowd wouldn't even listen to him. I told them . . . counterfeiters don't hang, they go to prison and someday they get out. Cullen laughed at me. He said he'd spent eleven years in prison and they could kill him before they'd ever take him back to one."

Fogarty idly watched the horsemen preparing to depart. Southward somewhere they would find their mules, but because evening was settling, they probably would not find them until after daylight tomorrow.

The pale-eyed man who rode the half-breed Mex saddle walked over, nodded to Elizabeth, and spoke to Marshal Fogarty. "A man rides up over a hill, and never knows what he's goin' to run into down the other side. You was after them all the time, an' they had this here

162

lady and those old gaffers prisoner. Marshal, my name's Walt Fraser."

Fogarty pumped the offered hand. "Joe Fogarty, Sheridan town marshal. This here is Elizabeth Durning. She's a Pinkerton detective. There's another lawman back up there somewhere; a deputy U.S. marshal out of Denver."

The pale-eyed man's gaze lingered on Fogarty for a long time before he wagged his head. "Well, we'd like to make it down yonder before it's too dark. You got any reason for us not to ride along?"

"Nope. And I'm grateful for your help. One question, Mr. Fraser: How'd you manage to shoot Booker?"

The horseman nodded. "One of the men come on to my hideout gun when he was goin' over me. He sort of half turned so's those gents up the slope couldn't see him real well and told me there was three of them, they had some prisoners includin' a lady, and that the law was close by somewhere, on their trail. That's all he had time to say. That's how I happened to have the gun when that feller got on my horse."

Fogarty felt for his makings. "Like I said, Mr. Fraser, we're real obliged to you an' your friends."

Fraser watched the quirley taking shape. "Marshal, we got a jug an' you sure look like a man who could use a pull off it."

For the first time in two days, Fogarty felt like smiling. "I appreciate it, Mr. Fraser. Maybe the next time we meet."

"Sure," assented the horseman, and turned to approach his companions, who were ready to depart. There were some calls back and forth, some hand salutes, and eventually only the faint sound of barefoot horses.

Dusk was passing. Reg Lee and James McGregor had pulled William Booker and Cullen Dowd to the west side of the road. There was nothing to cover them with, but the darkness would take care of that shortly.

McGregor confronted Joe Fogarty. "Good thing I asked them mule traders, or whatever they was, to tell Silas to send a wagon back for us, because no one else did."

Fogarty considered the gun maker. "If there's any grub, James . . . "

There was, not nearly enough, but after it was divided where the men hunkered on the east side of the road, the arrival of cool air inspired everyone to do something about the one factor they could indeed do something about.

They scrambled up the slopes and returned with armloads of deadfall tree limbs. They brought back enough to last the entire night, even though they did not expect to be marooned that long.

The federal deputy had removed everything from the pockets of the dead men. He held out a hand so that everyone could see a thick, round object with a pair of thumb-screw closures.

As McGregor reached for the thing, the deputy marshal said, "For makin' counterfeit silver dollars. Easy to hide, easy to use. Booker had it."

Hugh was leaning on his elbow, warm, relaxed, and best of all no longer being forced to hike along for miles with both arms lashed behind him. He jutted his stubbly jaw at the only prisoner. "How about him? What's in his pockets?"

Macy's face was badly swollen. There was a cut along his right cheekbone, and his lower lip had been split. It, too, was swollen. He refused to raise his eyes when Pepperdine mentioned him.

Reg Lee, the liveryman, who was sitting beside Macy, leaned slightly, and used a bony elbow to encourage the surviving outlaw to empty his pockets. He did. The only incriminating article in his possession was a tightly tied small packet of greenbacks. Reg untied the string, looked sourly at the notes, and raised his hand to pitch them into the fire when Macy squawked at him. "Not them! That's perfectly legitimate money. I been carryin' it for years in case I'd ever be in a place where I couldn't pass homemade money."

The liveryman held the notes to the fire, shrugged, and passed them around until they reached Joe Fogarty, who only indifferently examined the greenbacks before pocketing them.

As darkness increased, so did the cold. James and Hugh took the federal deputy back up the rearward slope and returned with more dry limbs. When they added to the pile that was already there, Hugh said, "That's enough wood to keep the fire goin' for two, three days."

McGregor scowled. "Maybe we'll be here that long. Maybe those mule traders'll get smoked up at Rusty's place and forget all about us."

Pepperdine had an answer for that. "You remember what Jack Carpenter said, you old badger? He'll be comin' back this way tomorrow."

A NIGHT TO REMEMBER

SOMEONE WOULD BE ALONG. SILAS WOULD PROBABLY send up a wagon, but as McGregor dourly said, with someone as stingy and just plain rank mean as Silas Browning, a man could never be sure.

They stoked the fire. It was all they had to hold back

the darkness, as well as the increasing chill. They were solicitous of Elizabeth Durning, who had not said much since the fight had ended. Old Hugh dragooned McGregor to climb back up among the trees on the east side of the road and fetch back bundles of fragrant pine boughs from which they fashioned a camp-bed. When she protested weakly, they insisted that she lie down and rest. She positioned herself so that her back was to the fire.

There was desultory conversation marked by long intervals of silence. Everyone was dead tired. The federal deputy marshal gave up questioning their prisoner and allowed Macy to stretch out. The men regarded the counterfeiter with expressionless faces, then ignored him as the deputy U.S. marshal lifted out the Lightning Colt he had retrieved after the fight and spoke in an offhand, detached manner like a man reasoning aloud with himself.

"The marshal up in Denver heard the Pinkertons was arming with these double-action guns and had a test made. What he came up with was that a person could fire off six rounds with one of these guns much faster'n someone else could empty the cylinder of a single-action."

None of the listening men appeared to consider the Lightning Colts in a very favorable light, but only one of them commented, and he was probably the most qualified among them to do so.

McGregor said, "Speed isn't what matters most, friend. The slug that went through our town banker came from one of those little guns. The feller who fired at him through a whittled hole in the wall had all the time in the world to pull the trigger—and the banker's still alive. But if that'd been a forty-five, or even a

166

forty-four caliber, the way he was hit, right now he'd be as dead as yesterday."

Charley Wright did not dispute any of this. In fact, his sole purpose in bringing the subject up was to denigrate Lightning Colts.

Joe Fogarty remembered something. "What happened to the Pinkerton lady's nickel-plated gun?"

The federal officer knew. "Macy put it in his saddlebags. I expect it's still in them, up yonder where we got set afoot." The federal officer also had a question of his own to ask. "How'd you get behind us, Marshal? They watched for someone after we reached the timber."

"Stayed in low places out of sight and kept on riding even after dark." As he finished speaking, Fogarty put a bland look upon McGregor and Pepperdine. "How did you know I was after them?"

Pepperdine spread both hands wide and made a raffish, sly smile when he replied, "Well, now, Joe, you left a wide trail, startin' with Jim Young an' endin' somewhere over yonder in the timber. We just rode Jack Carpenter's coach up a ways and cut inward to get ahead of Macy and his friends."

Fogarty eyed Pepperdine sardonically. "You an' Reg an' James got out and *walked* westward?"

The liveryman replied, "Yep. Accordin' to Hugh's figurin', them folks would have to rest their livestock an' maybe feel safe once they were in the trees, so they'd just poke along. All we had to do was walk west until we was in front of them . . . Pretty fair idea, wouldn't you say, Marshal? Well, that's exactly what we did; we walked until my feet liked to have dropped off. When we come on to a big trail over there, why, we just naturally picked out good ambushin' places and settled in to make the capture. Real fine plan, wouldn't you say? You'd be behind them, we'd be in front of them."

The longer Reg talked, the more bitter and sarcastic he began to sound.

"Well, now, Marshal, I found some old pockmarked big rocks and got set so's I couldn't see but in one direction, straight in front down the trail." Reg paused. Everyone but Macy and the Pinkerton lady was watching him. Hugh and James were beginning to look uncomfortable. Hugh made a point of pitching more wood onto the fire to make it hiss as sparks flew, but nothing was going to deter the liveryman, whose disgust had been increasing since his bad experience among the pockmarked rocks.

He raised his eyebrows in an exaggerated simulation of someone puzzled by the failure of such a brilliant plan. "There we was, Marshal, snug an' hid and waitin' for 'em, an' you know what happened?"

Fogarty did not reply. Neither did anyone else.

"I got someone's six-gun barrel shoved into the back of my neck. We was settin' there watchin' the down trail and they had already passed by, off to the west of the trail in among the trees. They was behind us, not in front of us.

"They heard us talkin'. Slipped back afoot and took each one of us like schoolboys playin' hide-an'-seek."

As he finished his recitation, the liveryman put a baleful stare on the hamessmaker, who was still very busy with the fire and did not return his look. But McGregor felt impelled to say something. "There wasn't anythin' wrong with the idea, Reg. How could we know they'd ride those horses half to death? Anyone else would have favored them, and then they would have been in front of us."

168

The liveryman glared, hung fire for a moment, then said, "James, if Gen'l Grant'd had you 'n Hugh on his staff, who do you expect would have won that damned war!"

The liveryman snorted, looked around for a place to stretch out, punched his hat into a pillow, and turned his back on the men who were silently and owlishly staring at him.

Heat loosened every muscle in Fogarty's body. His exhaustion was complete. He had not slept in a very long while. He followed the liveryman's example, stretched out, got as comfortable as it was possible to get on a hardpan roadbed, and slept.

They all slept, but the last pair to do so were the harnessmaker and the gunsmith. Pepperdine had his plug of molasses cured to comfort him; it did not take the place of the food his stomach craved, but, as he had said often, when a man was hungry, chewing tobacco beat hell out of a snowbank.

He was watching dancing flames when he said, "James, how long's it been?" and McGregor offered what he guessed was the only reply to the thought behind the question. "Long enough for that measly old bastard to hitch up a wagon all by himself and drive it up here."

"He's not coming, then."

James, too, leaned down to watch the flames. "Tomorrow. An' he'll have an excuse: Couldn't catch the horses, couldn't fling on the harness because his rheumatics was killin' him." He examined his swollen, chafed wrists and turned in the direction of the two dead men. "I've seen you do some crazy things, Hugh, but jumpin' up over the rump of that horse was the craziest."

169

Pepperdine spat into the fire, listened appreciatively to the frantic sizzling sound, and smiled at his old friend. "I didn't have a gun, and that renegade son of a bitch was goin' to shoot that mule trader."

McGregor looked up from the fire. He was as close to smiling as he ever came. He changed the subject. "That lady's tough as a boiled owl. Booker whined like a dog caught under a gate, even Cullen got to complainin', but by gawd she walked along without lagging back and never said a word."

Pepperdine nodded, jettisoned his cud, and straightened up from leaning on his arm. "I'll take the first watch," he said, and got a faint frown from his friend.

"Watch for what? There's Booker and Dowd. Macy couldn't stand up if he had help. What are you goin' to watch for? Go to sleep."

As he was speaking, James was placing more dry scantlings on the fire. It was almost too hot. The older men exchanged a grunt and settled against the ground. There were pinpricks of light above them by the millions. There was not even a breath of wind, which was unusual in a slot like this, where the only clear run the wind had in any direction was down the excavated roadway.

Sometime in the small hours, when the cold had reached its peak and the fire had died down, Charley Wright rose to place more wood on the coals, then went back to his bed ground after a long look around.

Nothing moved and there was not a sound, not even when four dog-wolves came to the very edge of the eastside bank and stood like carvings as they studied the unusual sight below them.

They did not make a sound when they withdrew,

either, but even if they had, it was doubtful that the dead-tired, slumbering people down on the road would have heard them.

They were still dead to the world when a sliver of pale light flashed out above the treetops. They might have slept another hour or two if Elizabeth Durning had not risen to go back up among the trees, where the wolves had been, in search of a creek or a spring, and, having found neither, returned to stoke up the fire. It was the crackling sound that awakened the men.

They regarded one another with shock. Late yesterday there had been too much activity for any of them to pay attention to the appearance of the others, and later, after nightfall had arrived, it had been too dark, and they had been tired. But this morning, with cold daylight to show each stain, each stubbled face with its lines and unwashed greasiness, everyone's reaction to the realization that if the others looked terrible they must look the same had a silencing effect.

McGregor left them to walk down the road. There were places down there where he could climb a bank and see southward for miles. Silas should have had someone on the way by now.

During his absence the men tried to cheer up the Pinkerton lady. She smiled dutifully for them, but to Joe Fogarty her forced cheerfulness was worse than if she had not made the effort.

Reg Lee and Charley Wright got Ernest Macy to sit up. He looked even worse this morning than he had looked the night before. Hugh's fury had left marks that, while they would eventually heal, would scar the outlaw for life. Oddly though, although speaking was difficult for him, he did not seem to be in very much pain. Behind their puffiness his eyes were bright and watchful, particularly when he looked at Hugh Pepperdine. The others he had reason to resent; Hugh Pepperdine he had reason to hate with a strong passion. Hugh would have killed him yesterday if he hadn't been restrained by those mule traders.

They kept the fire going even after the chill faded as sunlight finally reached down to the roadway. Marshal Fogarty left the camp now and then, but the last time he walked away northward he did not return even though everyone else had, including McGregor, who stoically reported that as far as he could see southward in the direction of Sheridan, there was no sight of a wagon, a coach, or even horsemen.

The federal deputy was fretful. He asked how far it was to town. When McGregor told him, he said that if he wasn't dog tired he'd walk down there, but he made no move to do it.

No one offered to do it. Feelings of abandonment and isolation were strong among them. Reg glowered each time someone mentioned Silas Browning, but, as Elizabeth Durning pointed out, they did not know that the mule traders had told anyone in Sheridan that they were up here. There was no way of knowing that the mule traders had even gone to Sheridan. Despite what they had said, they could just as easily have changed course and never entered town.

McGregor watched Pepperdine carve a cud off his tobacco plug, then faced Ernest Macy. They exchanged a long, sulfurous stare before the gunsmith said, "How long did it take you to whittle that hole in the wall from inside the dogtrot?"

Macy's reply was curt. "I didn't carve it; Cullen did."

McGregor thought about that for a moment before asking another question. "How did he manage to do it with folks passin' back and forth on the sidewalk?"

"He made the hole after nightfall."

McGregor seemed to accept that explanation because his next question was about something altogether different. "How did you get the Pinkerton lady and the federal deputy?"

Macy was holding a soiled bandanna to his face when he answered. "We knew somethin' was goin' on. I saw her leave the jailhouse by the back door. We talked about it, an' Bill Booker volunteered to watch her. When she started down the runway, he came back and told us. All three of us went down there by the same back alley." Macy lowered the handkerchief to examine it, then returned it to his face. "The lady and the deputy were talkin' up the runway not very far from the alley. We could hear everything they said." This time when Macy paused he did not lower the handkerchief; he put a bitter glare on Elizabeth Durning as he spoke.

"She was tellin' him one of them had better ride to the nearest town that had a telegraph office and send a message to the marshal's office up in Denver that we was down here."

Macy stopped speaking. His swollen lower lip was bleeding slightly. He placed the handkerchief over his mouth, and James McGregor put his head slightly to one side in a listening position and did not speak for a long time. Eventually he got to his feet and faced northward.

The liveryman also rose. The others appeared not to have heard anything, but Hugh Pepperdine stood up, too. He said, "It's a wagon, James."

The gunsmith contradicted that statement. "It's a stagecoach. You never could hear worth a damn."

Pepperdine ignored the insult, as he'd been ignoring other insults from his old friend for years. He spat out his cud, wiped his mouth on a filthy cuff, and barely nodded his head. "Jack Carpenter. He said he'd be back down today. Where the hell is Joe?"

No one answered. Right at that particular moment Fogarty could have taken wing and flown away. As the rattling, solid sound of a heavy vehicle grew louder, it occupied their thoughts to the exclusion of everything else because it represented the one thing in the world they needed most: deliverance.

The sound died almost completely when the oncoming stagecoach entered that low dip a half mile or so northward. They waited for the sound to return, and this time it was accompanied by one of Silas Browning's large, badly weathered but sturdy coaches swinging along behind a six-horse hitch.

Pepperdine gave McGregor a light blow on the back and smiled through his pepper-and-salt beard stubble. "Can you see if that's Jack up there?"

"It's Jack, an' Joe's settin' up there beside him. He must've met Jack up the road a ways."

Hugh was relieved that Joe had just been accounted for, but he had something else on his mind. None of them had eaten since the night before, and that had been a starve-out meal. Carpenter's outfit would put them back in town before dinnertime, and, more to the point, since Jack was a drinking man, he'd most likely have something with him that would alleviate their aches and pains until they reached town.

The stage slackened down to a slogging walk while its driver sat up straight looking ahead. Fogarty had told him most of what had happened, but Jack was not prepared for the sight he saw: filthy, gaunt, bedraggled men, and that husky handsome woman he'd admired so much, standing near a seated man whose face looked as though he'd been fed headfirst through a sausage grinder, and behind them, not entirely visible but visible enough, two dead men lying side by side in the morning sunlight.

Carpenter spoke to Marshal Fogarty. "That's old McGregor with Reg Lee an' Hugh Pepperdine standing near that woman with the curly hair and blue eyes."

Fogarty's reply was dry. "I told you who was down here."

"Yeah, but you didn't say what they looked like. The feller on the ground don't look like he'll make it on into town."

"He'll make it."

Carpenter hoisted a big boot sole to the binder handle but exerted no force on it until he was close enough to see every detail, then he did, and the rear-wheel blocks tightened against a steel tire as Jack called down to his horses as he eased back on the lines.

Dust rose beneath the stagecoach. As he leaned to loop the lines and climb down, he said, "Good thing all I got is light freight. If I'd had passengers an' they saw that bunch . . ." Carpenter did not finish the sentence as he stepped from the boot sling to the wheel hub and from there to the ground.

Joe Fogarty did not climb down right away. He glanced northwestward up the hill where he'd left his hobbled horse. It would make out all right. A hobbled horse could move around to find feed where a tied horse couldn't. He'd come back for it in a day or two.

NOT QUITE
BACK TO NORMAL

THERE WAS VERY LITTLE TALK ON THE RIDE DOWN TO Sheridan, mainly because the people riding inside had already pretty well talked themselves out and were too used up to make unnecessary conversation. Also, the person Carpenter'd had up there with him on the ride down to where the fight had occurred was now inside with the other passengers.

The pair of corpses was in the rear boot, out of sight, if not out of mind. Carpenter, like most conscientious whips, was never without a square green tin of collar-sore ointment that smelled of sheep fat and that cured, with almost miraculous efficiency, scratches, cuts, and rope burns like the ones McGregor had on each wrist.

James had slathered each wrist and had then buttoned soiled cuffs over them. Pepperdine was grudgingly pleased that Carpenter'd had something along to help his friend's injuries, and a long way from being pleased that Carpenter did not have a jug of popskull in his "possible kit," too.

The measure of anyone's exhaustion was whether they could sleep on a stagecoach. The best whips on earth could not control the pitching forth and back, nor the abrupt teethshaking staccato bumping when a stretch of washboard roadbed was encountered.

Also, even though there were coaches balanced over newfangled steel-leaf springs, Silas Browning's properly profit-minded outfit had neither adapted its older stages nor purchased any of the newer models, but used several dozen older, thoroughbrace models. The result was that along with the shiplike rolling, the forth and back pitching, Browning's big rigs yawed and rocked from side to side.

It was not uncommon for passengers to get "seasick" a thousand miles from the ocean. It was also uncommon for passengers to sleep, but Carpenter's riders did, all but Elizabeth Durning. She sat braced, expressionless, watching the countryside slide rearward. Her body relaxed to the jolting, and she looked detached from everything around her.

Joe Fogarty eyed her before falling asleep. When he awakened as the stagecoach slackened to the accompaniment of rattling harness, she was still sitting like that.

Fogarty leaned out a window, saw rooftops dead ahead, and settled back to jar his companions awake by kicking their boots. Reg Lee leaned to squint ahead. Over the noise of harness and steel tires grinding dust, he said, "There was times when I didn't figure I'd ever see Sheridan again." He looked balefully at Ernest Macy, who was holding a bandanna to his face again, leaned abruptly, felt for the canteen beneath the seat, and shoved it out as he growled, "Soak the cloth in water."

Macy did not say "thank you," nor did he look at the liveryman, but he soaked the cloth before placing it against his feverish face again.

Charley Wright nudged Hugh Pepperdine and jutted his chin in Elizabeth Durning's direction. Hugh nodded in silence. He, too, had been watching the handsome woman. So had McGregor, but if he'd felt any of the anxiety or the compassion of the harnessmaker and the town marshal, he didn't let it show.

The town was moving into its customary afternoon lull. There was a little traffic, mostly mounted men, and there were people on the sidewalks, but no one paid the slightest attention to the stagecoach. Joe Fogarty watched as they passed southward toward Browning's corralyard, saw Hugh eyeing him, blew out a big breath, and wagged his head.

Jack Carpenter made a wide turn, entered the dusty yard with two feet to spare on either gatepost, let the lines lie slack as yardmen appeared, and started climbing down. Old Silas appeared, wearing his huge old hat and scowling as the passengers alighted. He watched until they were all on the ground, then approached Marshal Fogarty to say, "You folks look like it was the truth."

Fogarty's stare at the old man was cold. "What was the truth?"

"What them mule traders was sayin' over at the saloon. Rusty sent a teller for me. Marshal, them mule traders was two-thirds drunk when I got over there. There's nothin' on the face of this earth more disgustin' than a drunk. They was tellin' the whole saloon about there bein' a big fight north of the water-box turnout. Folks gettin' shot, you up on a side hill shootin' it out with a renegade, horses running off . . . You never heard such a wild tale in your life."

Fogarty stared at the old man, almost spoke, paused for a moment, then grabbed Silas by the arm, dragged him around to the boot, and forced him to look in.

Browning made a squawking sound.

Fogarty released him and turned as Charley Wright and Reg Lee came up. The liveryman was scowling in disbelief. "He didn't even try to send no one?"

Fogarty shook his head and walked away.

Hugh and James were leaving the yard when Fogarty caught up with them. "Where's the Pinkerton lady?" he asked, and got a couple of indifferent answers. "Went up the road toward the rooming house," McGregor replied. Hugh said, "She didn't look real good, Joe."

They walked away, leaving Fogarty in the gateway until Charley Wright walked out with Ernest Macy. Without a word Fogarty led them down to the jailhouse. There the federal deputy marshal left, bound for the cafe across the road. Fogarty told Macy where to sit, then went to his desk to toss aside his hat, get comfortable in his chair, and regard the surviving outlaw.

"Where is your counterfeiting printing press?" he asked.

Macy did not even hesitate. "Up north in an old barn. Cullen was going to fetch it down here."

"Draw me a map on how to find it."

Macy nodded. "Yeah. As soon as you get the sawbones to patch me up, an' after you feed me."

Fogarty did not move. "Where were you goin' when you left town?"

"North."

"That'd be the worst possible direction for you. Someone would look for you up there."

Macy did not dispute this; he simply said, "That was a chance we had to take. We had to get the money-makin' equipment before anyone else got it. If we didn't have that, we couldn't keep going."

"What happened to the Pinkerton lady while you had her prisoner?"

"Happened? Nothin' happened to her except that she had to do a hell of a lot of walking. What makes you think anything happened to her? Did she tell you something did?"

"No. But something must have. She hasn't hardly opened her mouth since the roadway fight."

Macy shrugged. "Go ask her. Right now I need the sawbones and something to eat."

Fogarty locked his prisoner in a cell, then went over to the cafe. The place only had four or five other diners. The federal officer was not among them; he had filled up and departed. There were questions for the town marshal the moment he sat down at the counter. He ordered his meal as though he were deaf to the questions, made no attempt to answer any one until after hot coffee had arrived, then all he said was the bare minimum.

Up at Rusty Morton's bar, though, Reg Lee was handed a loaded jolt glass every time he paused to lick his lips. There were no less than fifteen townsmen hanging on every word he had to say about his experiences, beginning with the stagecoach ride northward and ending with the wild fight in the middle of the roadway. By morning Reg's story, with increasingly lurid embroiderings, would be all over town. By the day after, Reg might not even have recognized the story as it spread over the range beyond town.

Hugh and James ate at the cafe, sojourned to Morton's saloon, and, after a few shots of whiskey, went to their separate business establishments and bedded down.

Fogarty did the same; he was asleep within five minutes of going to bed. Whatever loose ends had to be cared for could wait.

In the morning he met Dr. Pohl at the cafe. It was too noisy for conversation, so they finished eating and went out front. Pete Donner was coming right along. It was still a minor miracle, in Henry Pohl's view, that anyone could recover so quickly and thoroughly from being shot through the body. Donner wanted to see Marshal Fogarty the moment he got back to town.

Fogarty did not say he would go up to the Pohl place. He mentioned the two dead men over in the corralyard, and the physician promised to work on them as soon as they were delivered to his embalming shed. He had questions that Joe patiently answered as best he could, then went down to Dennis's store for a sack of smoking tobacco and papers. He encountered Jim Young at the tobacco counter. Jim had heard several versions of what had occurred and complimented Joe Fogarty. He was particularly pleased that someone had killed Cullen Dowd. "He was goin' to shoot me sure as I'm standin' here. I don't like bein' told folks have been killed, but this time I do. How is the lady? She looked scairt pea-green up in my yard before they all taken off on them stolen horses. By the way, Marshal, a couple of fellers whose horses got stole was up to see me madder'n hell. All I could tell 'em was that when you got back you'd know what to tell them."

Fogarty went over to the tonsorial parlor, got a chunk of soap, a threadbare old towel, and the use of the bathhouse out back, all of it for only two bits.

He soaked in hot water until he began to feel normal again. Those stolen horses would show up. They always did in cattle country, where riders saw, and usually investigated, anything moving on their range.

When he got around to it, he'd write up the charges against Ernest Macy for presentation to the next circuit-riding judge who arrived in town. If Macy hadn't been such a pig-headed damned fool, Dowd and Booker more than likely would still be alive. Maybe not Cullen Dowd, but Booker would have been.

Then he laughed. Pepperdine, McGregor, and Reg

181

Lee *walking* through the mountains to ambush those fugitives. He also laughed about Hugh's wild leap onto the back of that horse to get at Macy.

When he was ready to leave the bathhouse, it was midday and there was a humid hush over the land. He did not notice the immense cloud galleons moving with ponderous grace from beyond the distant mountains until he had taken food over to Macy, who seemed capable of eating everything in sight and who also complained that the medicine man had not been to see him.

Fogarty had put off seeing the Pinkerton lady since he had awakened this morning. By now, though, he knew she had had plenty of time to rest, eat, get cleaned up, and feel normal again.

He had to pass Dr. Pohl's place on his way to the hotel, so he stopped in to ask Henry to look at his prisoner. He would have left after Henry's promise to go down to the jailhouse, but Pete Donner was in the parlor, recognized Fogarty's voice, and called to him.

Fogarty went as far as the doorway. He knew what was coming and did not anticipate it with pleasure. He'd been asked the details leading up to his confrontation with the outlaws by just about everyone he'd met over the past twenty-four hours. When Donner asked about the fate of the outlaws, the marshal told him that only Macy had survived. When Donner asked if steps had been taken to prevent anyone from using the same counterfeiting equipment again, Fogarty told him he hadn't yet done anything about that, but he would within the next day or two. Donner fixed Fogarty with his suspicious little dark eyes and said, "Is it true that woman who was in the bank the day I got shot was a Pinkerton detective?"

Fogarty nodded as he started to turn away. Donner was not quite finished.

"Did she get hurt, shot or anythin' like that, Marshal?"

"She didn't get shot, but she sure got put through the mill after the fugitives captured her."

"You're goin' to see her, are you, Marshal?"

"Yes. When I leave here."

"There's somethin' you could tell her. The bank didn't offer no reward and don't feel obliged to offer none. She wasn't hired by the bank."

Fogarty leaned in the doorway eyeing the banker. When he finally turned away, he said nothing, but out front on the porch with Henry Pohl, he put a question to the doctor. "How can you stand that son of a bitch, Henry?"

Pohl looked rueful. "Not very well, Marshal. My wife told me last night if I don't get him out of here soon she was going to hire a couple of men to carry him to his house whether I thought he was well enough to be moved or not."

"Is he well enough to be moved?"

"Yes. I think so. Of course, we've got to look in on him now and then for a while yet."

"Yeah. See you later, Henry."

"Take care, Marshal. Oh . . . there's something I wanted to ask you. I wrapped McGregor's wrists today, and he mentioned that that lady detective didn't look very well after she was freed from the fugitives. Have you seen her? Does she seem all right to you?"

Fogarty was already moving toward the roadway when he answered. "That's where I'm goin' right now, but no, Henry, she didn't look all right to me. After I've talked to her, I'll see if she'll come down here. I don't

183

think she was physically hurt, but after Booker and Dowd were killed and the smoke settled, she was white as a sheet an' acted like she didn't hear what was said to her. Like she didn't know where she was."

"Should I wait up, in case it's late when she comes to see me?"

Fogarty could not answer that question. "That'll be up to her. Good night."

After Marshal Fogarty was gone, Henry Pohl turned to reenter the house. He encountered his wife in the doorway. She was still looking at Fogarty striding along as she said, "Men! Of course that girl isn't all right." She did not step aside so her husband could enter the house. "You should go see her."

Dr. Pohl looked pained. "I can't just walk in on her and tell her she needs an examination."

His wife finally yielded, but as he marched past, she had one more thing to say. "Well, *I* can."

Henry turned slowly. "It's not up to us, it's up to her."

Dr. Pohl's handsome wife fixed him with a merciless stare. "You just get rid of Pete Donner, and leave her to me."

CLOUD GALLEONS

FOGARTY WAS APPROACHING THE HOTEL PORCH WHEN awareness of the humidity caused him to stop and raise his eyes. Those immense white clouds were especially noticeable. They were moving with ponderous slowness, but they were making sufficient headway to threaten the sun, and with them came a total lack of movement of air.

He reset his hat, instinctively thought the rain would be gratefully received out on the cow ranges, and entered the hotel.

He knocked lightly on Elizabeth Durning's door, waited, then knocked again. As he waited the proprietor came along, nodded curtly, and jerked his head rearward. "She's out back."

Fogarty walked the length of the hallway and saw her sitting alone in the shade of a swaybacked grape arbor. She looked as she had when he'd first seen her: crisp, sturdy, with shiny, short curly hair. Her back was to him until he opened the door and walked through humid sunlight to the arbor's fragrant shade, which was only marginally cooler than direct sunshine. He smiled as he pulled a little bench around and sat down. She offered no greeting and avoided looking at him. He studied her profile briefly; then hitched the little bench around where she could not avoid seeing him, as he said, "You look rested."

She barely inclined her head, still looking to one side of him.

He groped for other words for a while, then said, "It's finished. Macy'll give me directions to the barn up north where their counterfeiting equipment is. The federal marshal can find it and smash it. I got no idea when a circuit-riding judge will be along, not that it'll matter a whole lot. Macy needs some rest, too . . . Miss Durning?"

She brought her face slowly around to him. "That's the first time I ever saw anything like that, Marshal."

He held his hat in both hands, idly turning it. "I figured as much."

"Before, I did the planning, the organizing, the groundwork. I thought that someday something like that might happen. My supervisor told me it would if I remained with the agency."

185

"Yeah. But figuring something might happen someday an' bein' in the thick of it when it really did happen are two different things."

"Yes."

Fogarty looked at the hat in his hands. "I've got to go up yonder where they left their saddles and whatnot and bring those things back. Someone said your nickel-plated gun is in the saddlebags. I'll bring it back to you."

"I was no more than thirty feet from William Booker when that man shot him. I was looking straight at him. Last night I awakened several times seeing the expression on his face."

Fogarty stopped twirling the hat. "I can't tell you there won't be other nights like that, but I can tell you from experience that as time passes the vision becomes more detached, more sort of impersonal, like you're recallin' a picture you saw somewhere."

He had an increasing sense of outrage at whoever had sent her out to track down the outlaws. Before it could become real anger, reason told him that maybe whoever had sent her had done so particularly because counterfeiters were not normally as violent and deadly as other kinds of outlaws. He had actually been trying not to put her in the kind of situation she had lived through.

He would never know whether this was true or not. What he *did* know was that people who played with fire eventually got burned. People, male or female, who were professionally involved in enforcing the law, would sooner or later witness something approximating what she had survived up yonder where the stage-road fight had occurred.

He started to speak and she interrupted him. He said,

"Someday . . ." and that was as far as he got before she looked squarely at him and spoke. "Someday my life would be in danger. They impressed that on me, Marshal, and I accepted it. But with Macy and the others my life was never really in danger. There was hardship, but I'm physically fit and stay that way, so the walking didn't bother me very much."

He returned her steady gaze without blinking. "Ma'am, you're mistaken. Your life *was* in danger. At least two of those men would not have hesitated to kill you if they'd thought it advisable. Dowd and Macy."

Her gaze jumped away from his face and lingered beyond the arbor, where bees were noisily at work among some very tall flowers someone had planted years before and no one had taken care of since.

He admired her profile. "Elizabeth, you don't belong in this business." When her gaze swung swiftly back, Fogarty smiled a little as he continued speaking. "You're very good at it. I got to admit I didn't believe that at first. Mostly, I expect, because I never met a female peace officer before. But you pretty well figured things out. Maybe not some of the details, but the rest of it you did real good at." His smile lingered as their eyes held. "You're smart. Whatever they told you, or didn't tell you, I'll never believe you didn't realize that someday you were going to maybe either use the nickel-plated gun you own or see someone else use guns."

She stared steadily at him through an interval of silence during which the sound of bees among the flowers was very distinct. When she spoke, her voice was very soft. "You're right, Marshal."

He finished it for her. "But when it finally happened, you were looking straight at a man only a few yards away when he got shot an' killed, and *that* was something you'd never thought about."

He stood up still holding his hat. "I don't think you know Sheridan's doctor. His name is—"

"Henry Pohl. You're right, I don't know him, but I know who he is."

"Well, he's a mighty good man to talk to."

She looked up at him. He watched expressions come and go before she looked away when she said, "I'm sure he is . . . Marshal?"

"Yes'm."

"So are you."

A faint roll of thunder echoed down the vault of heaven, overriding the sound of bees. Fogarty glanced up. The cloud galleons were closer. Someone in the hallway was calling his name. He threw a gentle smile in the direction of the handsome woman and strode toward the caller.

It was Hugh Pepperdine. When Fogarty walked in, the harnessmaker craned for a look beyond, saw Elizabeth Durning sitting in the arbor, and shot Fogarty a quick look. "Is she all right?"

The marshal considered his answer before giving it. "Well, she will be."

The older man accepted that. "Yeah . . . A circuit-ridin' judge was just over at Rusty's place washin' the dust out of his gullet. Now he's down at your office."

They left the hotel together. They walked together down as far as the harness shop, where Hugh turned in. By the time Fogarty reached the jailhouse, the man who had been waiting for him was leaning in the open doorway smoking a fat cigar and studying the town. He nodded and moved aside without smiling as Marshal Fogarty came along. After a perfunctory greeting, the judge said, "I heard a pretty wild tale up at the saloon," and returned to the chair he'd left to stand in the doorway.

Fogarty told the story as it had happened, while His Honor considered the ragged, glowing end of his stogie. When Fogarty finished, the judge, who was a short, thick man with a pepper-and-salt beard and features like President Grant, put a gimlet-eyed stare upon the marshal as he said, "You got it all written up, have you?"

Fogarty hadn't. "No. But I'll do it right away."

His Honor arose with the cigar clamped between strong teeth. "I'll go set up for business at the firehouse like always. Marshal, if possible, I'd like to get this over with by evening. I got delayed up at Bluestem." Ash fell down onto the front of the judge, which he brushed off indifferently before continuing. "They had some horse thieves. It was a damned mess. No formal complaint filled out, four witnesses who'd got the town all fired up for a lynching." His Honor sighed. "Everybody yellin' at once." The judge smiled bleakly around his stogie. "I been thinkin' about retirin'. I'm gettin' a mite long in the tooth for saddle backin' all over hell and havin' to listen to idiots. Well, when you're ready, I'll be waitin'."

Fogarty waited until the judge had departed before sitting down to start writing. This was the part of his job he disliked the most. He could tell someone all the details of a crime a lot easier than he could put them down on paper.

The rain came. Not with a light drizzle like most rains did, but all of a sudden, with drops the size of spur rowels striking the roadway with enough force to make puffs of dust spurt upward like miniature explosions.

Fogarty paused to listen. Maybe the range cattlemen

189

would be delighted, but folks in town wouldn't be. For one thing, if a rainfall lasted very long Main Street became a chocolaty millrace, merchants wrung their hands, and everything dwindled, including trade and daylight and warmth.

Henry Pohl arrived at a run, carrying his little black satchel. He was breathless. He was also damp, although most of the stores he'd passed on his way down to the jailhouse had overhangs out front. Heat warped the boards, so while the overhangs might offer some relief from hot sunlight, they leaked like sieves.

The marshal abandoned his desk to take Henry down into the cell room where he could examine Ernest Macy. The outlaw still looked badly swollen and discolored, but otherwise he seemed well enough as Fogarty unlocked the cell door for Henry, then relocked it and returned to his office where the full force of the storm made more noise on the roof than a whole battalion of drummers.

Two horsemen in the middle of the road were riding at a kidney-damaging trot southward toward the protection of Reg Lee's barn. They were humped over and soaked.

Fogarty had been back working on his formal complaint for ten minutes when the door was flung inward for the second time. His Honor stepped inside, shook like a dog, removed his hat to dump water from the crown, and scowled at Fogarty as though he were somehow responsible for the downpour. Over the noise, His Honor said, "You got it finished, Marshal?"

Fogarty's eyes widened. "I just got started."

"Well, in fifteen minutes ain't a soul goin' to be able to cross that road without a boat. I got no choice but to get a room for the night at the hotel and hope to hell it lets up by tomorrow. They usually do, these summertime cloud bursts." His Honor's scowl lifted. "You go ahead and finish writin' it up, an' we'll hold court in the morning-providin' the storm's at least down to a decent rainfall."

His Honor turned, reset his hat, checked to be sure his coat was buttoned to the gullet, and walked back out into the roadway.

Fogarty threw down his pencil, crossed to the doorway, and leaned to look northward. Water was descending in tiers, one behind the other. There was not a soul in sight except the judge, and he was not scuttling in the direction of the hotel. He was wading through slush on a diagonal course for Rusty Morton's saloon.

Fogarty watched him disappear into Rusty's waterhole, then closed the door and started back for his desk, changed his mind because by now the doctor should have done all the patching he could do on Macy, yanked back the steel-reinforced oaken cell-room door, and walked down there. It was as dark in the cell room in midafternoon as it would normally have been at eight o'clock at night.

He paused midway to light the hanging lamp and place it back on its ceiling hook. It was not enough light, but it was better than no light.

He only glanced in the cell as he leaned to insert the door key. Both Ernest Macy and Dr. Pohl were facing him, motionless and silent. Macy was slightly behind and to one side of the doctor.

When Fogarty swung the door wide, its customary grating sound was lost in the more thunderous noise of the overhead rain.

Both his prisoner and the doctor were staring straight at Fogarty. He started to enter the cell. An instinctive warning stopped him dead still. Macy pushed Henry Pohl forward a couple of steps. He was holding the doctor from the back. He had to raise his voice to be heard as he said, "Drop the six-gun, Marshal, an' kick it over to me."

Fogarty did not move. His stare met the doctor's eyes.

He recognized the look he was getting and slowly sank into a slouch. "Did you have a gun in your satchel, Henry?"

The doctor also had to speak loudly. "No. He's got my surgical shears."

Fogarty's attention returned to his prisoner. "Scissors?"

Macy held his right hand away briefly so that Fogarty could see his grip on the shears. They were long and tapered. When closed they measured about six inches. He was gripping them like a knife, and when he pushed them back out of sight, Henry Pohl winced.

Fogarty regarded the outlaw for a long moment before speaking. "You're crazy. That's not goin' to work."

Henry Pohl winced again. This time he also made a short gasp as the daggerlike tips of the shears pierced his clothing and drew blood.

Macy's retort to the lawman was short. "They're long enough to cut him all to hell inside. Kick your gun over to me, or you're goin' to be responsible for his killing. I won't be. I'm offerin' him an' you a chance. I'm not goin' to prison, Marshal. Not after what Cullen told us it was like. Kick the gun over here, or I'll bury these shears to the hilt in his back . . . Marshal, you know what folks'll say if you force me to kill him? That his death was your fault."

Joe Fogarty stood in his slouch just inside the cell with

guttering, weak lamplight around him. The storm was rising to a crescendo that might last all night, and if it did, Sheridan was going to be ankle-deep in water by morning. Roads would be impassable, visibility would be just slightly more than arm's length. Whether or not Macy made it through the night on horseback, it would be impossible to track him or, for that matter, to even see him if the storm continued through the following day.

Henry Pohl gritted his teeth and flinched as the outlaw stuck him again.

Fogarty straightened up. He could kill Macy with one shot, but the moment his right hand dipped, Macy could plunge the shears into the doctor's back.

This was no Mexican standoff. Macy meant exactly what he had said.

DEATH HAS MANY FACES

FOGARTY KICKED THE SIX-GUN TO WITHIN REACH OF the desperate man and did not take his eyes off Macy as he squatted very slowly, looking straight back at the town marshal when he groped for the weapon. As he straightened up, a lot of the tightness left his face. He looked almost exultant. He flung the scissors aside and gestured with the six-gun for Fogarty to lead the way up the corridor, which Fogarty did, being careful to do nothing that Macy might interpret as threatening.

The light was better in the office, but the storm's sound was just as loud when Macy ordered both his prisoners to lie facedown on the floor.

Fogarty held the outlaw's gaze for a moment and wagged his head but did not speak as he got flat down. Dr. Pohl did the same.

Macy searched for shackles but did not go into the storeroom where they were hanging. Fogarty hoped very hard that he would extend his search to that area, because then both he and Henry Pohl would be out of Macy's sight.

But the outlaw did no more than glance at the storeroom door before moving to lash the ankles of his prisoners with belts, tie their wrists in back with bandannas, and stand briefly regarding them before taking down an old hat and jacket from a wall peg. While putting them on he raised his voice above the noise on the roof to say, "Yell your hearts out. No one'll hear you."

He left the jailhouse in a hurry, passing through the back room where the manacles and leg irons hung without even seeing them. He left the alleyway door open. Fogarty felt the rush of wet air as he was rolling toward Henry Pohl. "Use your teeth," he yelled, and maneuvered his body until the medical practitioner could go to work on the bandanna.

It did not take long. Fogarty sat up when his arms were free, fumbled rapidly to free his ankles, and sprang up. He wasted a minute or two slashing the doctor's wrist binding, then filled his holster from a drawer. He did not bother unlocking the chain that was threaded through the trigger guards of his rack-up long-barreled guns, but shrugged into his jacket, picked up his hat, and without looking back ran out into the alley.

Macy was not in sight, but visibility was extremely limited. There were deep boot-tracks in the mud pointing Southward. Within fifteen minutes they would disappear, but Fogarty had seen enough to conjecture that Macy was heading for Reg Lee's horse barn. He hastened along, pausing only occasionally to kick off balls of adhesive mud.

The sky was almost black, and while the storm was directly overhead, it surely had limits, even though as far as anyone in Sheridan could see in all directions there was no sign of a paled-out gray edging.

The noise was very loud where wagon loads of water struck rooftops. Later, Fogarty would reflect that he'd never seen such a thunderous downpour before.

But as he was approaching the rear of Lee's barn, he was not even very conscious of the waterlogged weight of the jacket he was wearing.

Unless Reg'd a saddled horse tied inside, Macy would still be in the barn, probably about ready to mount up and flee. It required about as much time to lead out a horse and rig it as it had taken for Fogarty to get free and rush down here.

He drew the wet gun, ran a soaked palm over his shirt inside the jacket to dry it, gripped the weapon, and eased around the north side of the barn's rear doorless opening.

It was dark in the runway up as far as the harness room. Up there, a solitary coal-oil lamp was guttering fitfully, giving off visible puffs of greasy smoke and swaying on its suspension wire.

There was no one in sight and no tethered animal waiting to be saddled. Fogarty squeezed around the doorjamb, got inside where the noise was louder, and began a slow stalk, pausing often, seeking movement. What he eventually saw, about the time he was halfway up the runway, was Reg Lee coming out of his harness room yanking an old hat furiously forward. He stopped to look in the direction of the roadway where those waves of water were following one another like soldier ranks, then started to turn farther as a stocky, disheveled man emerged from the harness room directly behind him, holding a cocked Colt kidney-high to the liveryman.

Something was said, but Fogarty could not hear the words as he inched to his right, feeling for an open stall door. He found one empty stall and faded into its darkness.

Reg was prodded down the runway. There were six or eight animals about equally distributed in stalls on both sides of the runway. Fogarty pressed deeper into darkness as they approached. Reg finally pointed and veered toward a particular stall, roughly opposite the empty one where Fogarty was hiding.

This time when the men spoke loudly Fogarty heard every word. The liveryman stood stiffly in front of a stall door as he said, "That's him. The toughest, strongest animal I own."

Macy snapped back, "Lead him out. Goddammit, you better move faster'n you been moving. I'll blow your head off!"

Reg shanked the horse, led him back up to a tie post in front of the harness room, and, with Macy following his every move like an armed shadow, brought forth the outfit. Without visible haste, but with what amounted to the same thing—lifelong experience at rigging out saddle animals— Reg did not make a single wasted motion.

Fogarty watched everything, and when Reg turned impassively to hand over the reins, he moved closer to the open door of his hiding place.

Macy yanked the big bay horse around. The animal turned stiffly, as if it were unaccustomed to this kind of treatment. Macy was preparing to mount when Reg yelled at him, "You better use spurs. You can drum all day on his ribs with slick heels an' he won't do no more'n trot."

Macy stood poised to mount. "Get a pair, dammit," he yelled. "Be damned awful sure that's all you bring out of the harness room with you. *Move!*"

When Reg returned, Macy was already in the saddle. Without looking up, Reg buckled one spur into place, went around, and buckled the other one into place. Then he stepped back, still bleakly impassive as Macy evened up his reins and leaned. The big bay horse had both ears turned back waiting for the slightest signal. The moment Macy leaned, he started toward the soggy roadway. At the same moment, Fogarty sprang into the runway, rushing ahead. He was ready to yell, had his gun raised and cocked, when Reg moved squarely in front of him, watching the outlaw leave the shelter of his barn.

Fogarty yelled at Reg to get the hell out of the way and started loping forward. Lee turned, stared briefly, then lunged hard and knocked Joe Fogarty off balance. As the lawman fought to catch his balance, the liveryman yelled at him, "You'll hit my horse! Dammit, put up that gun!"

Fogarty had both feet squarely in position when he snarled and would have aimed again, but Reg Lee struck his gun arm, forcing it upward. At the same time he placed his thick body directly in front of the town marshal and yelled at him again, "Stop it! I said, stop it!"

Macy was gone. He had turned southward in the roadway and was no longer visible. Fogarty was red-faced. He aimed a powerful blow that struck the liveryman in the shoulder, spinning him toward the wall, and raced for the front barn opening.

There was no horseman out there. He could have been no more than two hundred feet down the road and he still would have been invisible.

Fogarty stood in the downpour, gun hanging at his side, breathing hard and furious when Reg walked up gingerly massaging his shoulder. Fogarty refused to acknowledge his presence until the liveryman said, "You want that son of a bitch? Put up that damned gun and follow me."

Fogarty grabbed cloth as Reg would have moved past. He whirled Lee back around. "Are you crazy?"

Lee regarded the furious lawman almost blandly. "Yeah, probably, but if you'd fired in that kind of light you'd more'n likely have killed my big bay horse. Joe, you want to stand out here an' drown, or do you want to come along with me and catch that son of a bitch?"

Fogarty's eyes narrowed to slits. "He's gone."

"He sure is. Come along. We'll find him down the pike a ways."

"You *are* crazy, Reg."

"No. Not me. My big bay horse. There isn't a man alive can stay on top of him if he's wearin' spurs and gouges him with them. Come along, dammit."

Lee was right, but they had to kick off mud for almost a quarter of a mile before they found Ernest Macy. He was lying on his side with one leg cocked halfway over the other leg. He was dead. There was no sign of the big bucking horse.

Impassively, Reg knelt in mud to remove the spurs he'd deliberately buckled to Macy's boots, then stood up dangling them. He said, "Broke his damned neck. Look at the unnatural angle of his head. Well, there's your outlaw. Joe . . . just how the hell did he happen to come runnin' into my barn with a gun in his hand?"

Fogarty made sure Macy was indeed dead, retrieved the gun Macy had taken from him, nudged the liveryman, and pointed. Reg took Macy's ankles and

Fogarty took his arms. They struggled back the way they had come, dumped the outlaw in a horse stall, then leaned on the wall panting like they'd run a country mile.

While they were doing that, the big bay horse meandered up the runway from out back, and Reg went over to it to remove the rigging. He talked to the bay horse like he might speak to a child.

Fogarty waited until the animal had been returned to its stall before asking a question. "That's why you told him he'd need spurs?"

Lee nodded almost wearily. "Yeah."

"Why do you keep that horse, Reg? Someday he'll kill someone else."

"Naw, he won't. I ride him all over the countryside. He'll do anything you want him to do. He's easy to catch, is a good keeper. I wouldn't trade him for a farm in Missouri." Lee grinned a little, the first expression he'd shown since he'd been startled half out of his wits when Macy appeared in his harness-room doorway. "You could put a ten-year-old kid on him. You could trust your wife with him—if you had one. Just don't never even *think* about gettin' on that horse when you're wearin' spurs." Lee stopped speaking and smiling.

Fogarty used a soggy sleeve to wipe water from his face, shook his head, and started back toward the alley. Behind him the liveryman called out, "You do somethin' about him, Joe. I don't want no corpses in my barn. It's bad for business. You hear me? *Joe!*"

Fogarty replied just short of reaching the alleyway. "As soon as it lets up a little, I'll haul him up to Henry's embalmin' shed."

Henry Pohl was no longer at the jailhouse when Fogarty paused out back to use a flat stick on his boots before going through to his office. But in something like fifteen minutes Hugh Pepperdine and James McGregor arrived wearing old ponchos and carrying carbines. Henry had told them of Macy's escape. They eyed the soaked lawman in stony silence until he said, "He's dead. Down the road a few hundred yards. The horse Reg fixed him up with bucked him off an' he busted his neck when he landed."

Fogarty rummaged through several drawers before finding his whiskey bottle. With Hugh and James staring, he tipped back his head, swallowed three times, then extended the bottle. James drank first. Hugh took a long pull and placed the bottle atop the desk as he said, "Where is the body?"

"In a stall down at Lee's barn."

Fogarty sank down at his desk. Until this moment he had not noticed the squishy sound his feet made inside his boots when he moved. The coat he had shed was soaked through. So were his trousers. Even his hair was plastered down. He found a dry cloth in a drawer and mopped himself off as he said, "Now it's over for a damned fact. That circuit rider can leave town any time he wants to. There won't be a trial."

Pepperdine swept his poncho up in back and sat down as he spoke. "Leave town? Not unless he's got a rowboat."

Fogarty ignored that. "I never got the map from Macy where they hid their counterfeiting equipment up north. "He shrugged. "That's up to the U.S. marshal in Denver. He'll find it. If he don't . . ." Fogarty finished drying off and gazed from one old man to the other. "That's the last time Henry goes into one of my cells by himself, an' even then I'll go over him for anything sharp."

James had a comment to make. "Don't jump on Henry. He feels real bad. Bad enough without you raggin' him. He told us what happened when he dragooned us to help him steer Pete Donner to his house . . . an' Henry's wife give us both a peck on the cheek . . . Joe?"

"What?"

"Can you swim?"

Fogarty scowled at the gunsmith. "No, I can't swim. Why?"

"It's suppertime. The cafe's across the road, an' if you cross over with us—where there was wagon ruts there's washouts a foot deep. By now maybe two feet deep." McGregor went to stand in the doorway. Opposite the jailhouse Hank Dennis and Jack Carpenter were preparing to hurl a heavy rope across the millrace to several townsmen on the opposite side. As James watched, they made three attempts without success. The fourth time, though, Carpenter put all his rather considerable strength into the toss. Townsmen caught the rope, and James turned to say, "Let's go eat. They got a rope for us to hang on to. Hugh, what are you waitin' for?"

"My boots leak."

Absolutely pragmatic, James McGregor looked at the marshal and his old friend with a flinty stare. "You two goin' to set there because you might get wet?"

Fogarty went after his leaky hat and his sodden jacket and followed Hugh out of the building.

They were the first to use the rope, and while scarcely a soul appeared on the plank walks to watch, there were a lot of spectators behind store windows waving encouragement, including the dour cafeman who held the door open for them when they got across.

MAKING A WAGER

FOGARTY AWAKENED THE FOLLOWING MORNING TO A pair of unexpected phenomena. One, he, who hadn't had a cold in ten years, had the sniffles. The second phenomenon was that the sun was shining dazzlingly from a scrubbed-clean sky and the only sounds of water were off roof eaves and from the center of Main Street, where several creek-deep runnels still carried muddy water through town.

By the time he had donned clean, dry clothing, washed up out back, shaved, and was on the porch of the hotel breathing deeply of air as sweet smelling as new-mown hay, people were abroad in considerable numbers. Planks had been placed atop the mud so that womenfolk could cross Main Street without getting bogged down. Hank Dennis was standing out front of his store puffing on a cigar and warmly greeting every customer who turned in there. Rusty Morton was shoveling silt off the plank walk in front of the saloon, and Silas Browning, wearing his oversized old hat and looking more ludicrous than usual, was bawling orders at the yardmen who Marshal Fogarty could not see behind the palisaded gates.

Fogarty needed meat, potatoes, hot coffee, and a smoke. His town was a mess, but merchants and others would not permit it to remain like that very long. By afternoon, or as soon as the mud firmed up enough to support big horses and wagons, Reg Lee, among others, would begin hauling dirt to fill the deep roadway ruts.

A sturdy older man, wearing a wrinkled Prince Albert coat and black pants to match and using both arms like he was on a tightrope, crossed the duckboards with a cigar jutting at an unnatural angle. When he reached the west plank walk he removed the stogie, spat into the mud, plugged the cigar back between his teeth, and marched straight toward Marshal Fogarty. When he halted, he did not remove the cigar; he spoke around it. He clearly was not in a good mood.

"Well, sir, Marshal. I expect you got the damned complaint written up so's we can get this damned trial over with."

Fogarty smiled blandly. "No, sir, Your Honor, I don't have it written up."

The judge removed his cigar. "You don't have. I told you yestiddy I'm runnin' behind schedule."

"Yes, sir, you sure did."

"Well, now, that old gnome who runs the stage line told me at the cafe this morning he'd have a southbound ready to leave Sheridan within the hour."

"You can be on it, Judge."

His Honor regarded Marshal Fogarty in silence for a long moment, his pouched, shrewd little eyes as cold-appearing as creek pebbles. "Can I now? You want to keep this damned outlaw an' feed him until the next time I'm down here, do you?"

"He's dead."

The judge blinked.

"He broke out of jail last night during the storm, got a horse, and made a run for it. The horse bucked him off and broke his neck, an' if you'll excuse me, I got to get a couple of friends to help me haul his carcass up to the doctor's embalming shed."

Fogarty stepped past the grizzled older man and kept on walking until he reached the harness shop. Fortunately, the gunsmith was having coffee with the harnessmaker. Fogarty declined Hugh's offer of coffee and asked if the pair of them would pack Ernest Macy from Lee's horse stall up to Henry Pohl's shed across the alley from the doctor's house.

There was a pause during which McGregor and Pepperdine exchanged a look. Fogarty fished for a crumpled greenback, which he placed atop the counter, and waited.

Two pairs of aging eyes moved over to the greenback, met again, then James McGregor said, "How soon?"

"Soon as you can. With the sun gettin' hot and all . . ."

McGregor understood. "All right. By the way, did you know Silas is sending out a southbound this morning?"

Fogarty knew. "Yes. If Carpenter's toolin' it, it won't get stuck or break any wheels."

The old men exchanged another look. "He's drivin' it," Pepperdine conceded, and looked down into his two-thirds-empty coffee cup. "I guess it'll be travelin' light. Just one passenger an' no freight."

Fogarty was moving in the direction of the door when he responded. "Yeah, I know. That circuit-ridin' judge will be aboard."

Pepperdine and McGregor eyed Marshal Fogarty. One of them said, "Is that a fact? I didn't know that."

Fogarty was in the doorway by now. "I just talked to him up the road. He told me he'd bought passage."

"Well, then, there'll be two passengers, won't there?"

Fogarty looked back irritably. "How the hell would I know?"

Old Pepperdine remained unruffled when he replied, "You wouldn't, I guess. James met her in front of the corralyard office on his way over here a while back. She'd just paid for a ride south."

Joe Fogarty stood in the doorway gazing back at them both. "The Pinkerton lady?"

McGregor's inclination toward dourness prompted him to say, "That judge don't have a wife, does he?"

Fogarty moved clear of the doorway looking northward. Someone had set a heavy carpetbag on the hotel porch. While he was standing there, Elizabeth Durning appeared with the hotel proprietor, who, for once, was being both mannerly and helpful. Fogarty started back up there.

When the hotelman went back inside, a second man appeared. He was carrying a rangeman's possible bag and bedroll. It was the federal deputy from Denver, Charley Wright. He and Elizabeth Durning were talking to each other, and neither of them noticed the town marshal until his shadow fell nearby. Charley Wright nodded his head. "Morning, Marshal. We were just saying we figured it'd be a few days before you could go back up yonder where the Macy bunch had to leave their outfits. Her six-gun and some things they made me take out of my pockets are in the saddlebags up there. Maybe you could mail them to us."

Joe Fogarty agreed that it would be a few days. He assumed, correctly, that they had heard of Macy's last horseback ride when he said, "The ground's too wet now, but maybe by tomorrow it'll firm up enough to dig their graves. When Macy made his run for it, I thought he was more crazy than desperate, but maybe not, because if that horse hadn't dumped him, he most likely would have got clean away."

Elizabeth Durning was dressed in something made for traveling. It fit her very well, and it was sort of dove-gray. It wouldn't show dust the way something black or dark brown would. She returned Fogarty's gaze when

205

she said, "Dr. Pohl's wife visited me last night. We had to yell to be heard. She's a wonderful woman, Marshal. She said very candidly that Macy's escape was her husband's fault."

The marshal shifted stance. "Mostly it was my fault, but he's tended to other prisoners over the last couple of years, carrying that little black satchel with him, and Macy was the first prisoner to feel desperate enough to do what he did. One thing is a plumb fact, Elizabeth: No one, Henry or anyone else, will go into one of my cells again carrying anything that I haven't searched first."

She smiled at him. "My aunt once told me that there is a lesson to be learned from everything we do."

He smiled back. "I expect she was right. Have you folks had breakfast?"

Charley Wright had. He also had not paid for passage on the morning southbound yet, so he was fidgeting a little when he said. "I ate early. She hasn't, an' I better get down to the corralyard to pay for my stage ride."

As he left them carrying his bedroll, Marshal Fogarty said, "The cafe's probably empty now. Most folks who eat breakfast down there did so hours ago. Would you . . . ?"

"Will my satchel be all right here?"

He stepped over to lift it as he replied, "I'd guess it would be, but just to be safe we'll leave it at the jailhouse."

When they had put the carpetbag in Fogarty's office and were navigating one of those duckboard crosswalks, someone up north was standing in front of the corralyard yelling about something. Neither Elizabeth Durning nor Marshal Fogarty heeded the noise. Today Sheridan had plenty of noise.

The cafeman was rewarded for having shaved this morning by the arrival of the handsome woman with the
206

curly short hair and eyes as blue as cornflowers. He joked with them both, was almost courtly, and when he went behind his kitchen curtain to make up their breakfast platters, Joe Fogarty watched him until he was out of sight, then looked back with a sigh. Fogarty had been eating at the cafe since his arrival in Sheridan, and this was the first time he'd seen the cafeman other than taciturn, unsmiling, and sour.

By the time they had finished their meal, Fogarty had made another discovery: The cafeman could really cook, could actually turn out a delicious meal. As they rose to depart and Fogarty put silver coins beside his plate, he complimented the cafeman, who acknowledged the praise by completely ignoring Fogarty and smiling at Elizabeth Durning as he said, "Ma'am, I'm right pleased you enjoyed it. If there was someone like you in this town to cook for, it'd be a real pleasure to own a cafe."

As they were turning to depart, the marshal heard the high call he knew by heart, and before they had reached the front walkway, Jack Carpenter wheeled past without looking left or right as he either avoided or straddled roadway washouts. One passenger leaned out on the near side and waved. Deputy U.S. Marshal Charley Wright.

Elizabeth Durning stood like stone watching the stage bucket along toward the lower end of town, then slowly turned back as Fogarty said, "That darned old goat. He knew you wanted to be on the morning southbound."

She said, "The driver?"

"No. Silas Browning. The old curmudgeon who runs the company."

Her expression remained serene. "The same man who didn't send a wagon for us after the fight up the road?"

"The same. Come along. He'll put you on the next

stage if I got to wring his scrawny neck."

She said nothing until they had safely navigated the duckboards and were in front of the jailhouse, then, as Fogarty went inside for her satchel, she said, "Marshal, don't be upset."

He was standing just inside the office doorway with her carpetbag in his hand when he replied, "He knew. That's his cranky darned nature. He's a spiteful old . . ."

She took the satchel from him and put it down. "There'll be an evening stage, won't there?"

"Yes. But . . . "

"We could wait for it, couldn't we?" She went to a chair and sat down watching him. "Dr. Pohl's wife asked me to lay over and have supper with them tonight."

Fogarty stood like a stump. He was indignant, but he was also uneasy. In his lifetime he'd very rarely encountered a situation that wasn't explainable by horse-sense logic. Right now, with the handsome woman relaxed and half smiling up at him, he had an uncomfortable feeling that something was happening that would elude his best efforts to define it.

He went to a bench and sat down. He gazed at the chained weapons in the wall rack. "I'll go up an' talk to the hotelman, get you the use of your room until evening."

She, too, considered the gun rack. "It's a very nice town, Marshal. There are some likable people in it, and I'm glad I missed the stage."

"That was my fault for taking you down to the cafe. Well, partly my fault. Maybe half my fault and half Silas Browning's fault, the old weasel."

"I . . . really didn't want to be on that stage, Marshal."

He looked at her. Her profile was to him as she

208

studied the gun rack. For one second his heart faltered, then he said, "You didn't? I got to tell you I didn't want you to be on it."

Her blue gaze drifted back to his bronzed face. "Why?"

Fogarty felt sweat on his palms. "Well . . . I guess you don't want to talk about everything that's happened since you came here. But if you did, someday, we could sure spend a day or two doin' it."

Her soft gaze did not waver. "Dr. Pohl's wife said that if I'd lay over and have supper with them this evening, she'd invite you, too."

Fogarty studied the gun rack again. "She did?"

"Yes."

"Well, but you was packed and ready to leave."

"I was packed, Marshal."

He raised his hat to scratch vigorously and reset it. Any other time old Hugh, McGregor, maybe Reg Lee, or someone else would have come barging in by now. She'd said she was packed. She hadn't said she'd been ready to leave town. He let his breath out in a silent sigh. "Elizabeth."

"Yes."

"About bein' a Pinkerton detective . . ."

"Charley had my resignation in his pocket when he left this morning. He'll mail it from Denver."

Fogarty felt great relief. "That's the best thing I've heard in a long time. It's . . . just not something a woman ought to be doing."

"I know that now, but for a long time I didn't think that way . . . Joe?"

"Yes."

"Will the countryside be dry enough tomorrow for us to take a buggy ride?"

"I expect so," he replied, feeling color coming into his face. "You . . . don't want to leave Sheridan just yet?"

"No. Joe, I owe you a lot."

"No, ma'am. You don't owe me anything. Maybe it's the other way around."

She considered the hands in her lap without really hearing him. *Men! Strong as oak and twice as thick!* She did not raise her head when she said, "Can I leave my satchel here?"

"As long as you like."

She stood up. "Do you know Dr. Pohl's wife's first name?"

"Eleanor."

"Yes. I think I'll go up and visit with her." As he, too, rose, her eyes settled on his face again. "Shall I tell her you'll come for supper tonight?"

He thought his face was beet-red. It felt that way, but actually he was too bronzed for color to show. "Yes'm. I'd be real happy to do that this evening. Would it be all right for me to come by the hotel for you first?"

She smiled. "Yes, and in that case I'd better take the satchel with me and get my room back." She picked up the carpetbag and moved to the doorway, where she said, "Joe?"

"Yes'm."

"I think it sounds better to call me Elizabeth rather than ma'am."

"Yes'm." he replied, and watched her move out into the brilliant sunlight.

Later, as he was making a round of the town and stopped in at Rusty Morton's saloon, Pepperdine and McGregor were marveling at Rusty's latest acquisition, a spanking new brocaded vest straight from New York

210

City, and called upon Fogarty to examine the fine detail of the pattern and cloth.

The marshal leaned on the counter as Rusty preened like a peacock. "Cost seven dollars," he exclaimed. Fogarty considered the vest. Seven dollars was half what a rangeman made a month, a hell of a price to pay for something a man couldn't wear in the rain.

Fogarty stared at the vest as he said, "What color would you call those blue doodads on the front?"

Rusty didn't hesitate. "Cornflower blue."

Fogarty continued to lean. "I never saw anything as pretty as that color. Cornflower blue."

Hugh Pepperdine's forehead wrinkled slightly as he stared at the town marshal. He had a sudden hunch, and to test its validity he said, "Joe, that's not a real common color. Did you ever see it before?"

Fogarty turned slightly and smiled at the harnessmaker. "About an hour ago."

As he walked out of the saloon, Pepperdine leaned close to his friends and lowered his voice to a raspy whisper. "I'll tell you something. That Pinkerton lady missed the stage this morning."

McGregor saw nothing odd about this. "What of it? Folks been missin' stages since—"

"Let me finish, you old goat," the harnessmaker said. "Her and Joe Fogarty had breakfast together at the cafe, then they sat in his office for a long time. I know for a fact that cowboy-lookin' U.S. deputy marshal left town, an' her an' Henry Pohl's wife are gettin' thick as thieves."

As Pepperdine straightened up off the bar, McGregor fixed him with one of his bleak looks as he said, "What the hell are you tryin' to say—if anything?"

Hugh considered the other two men over a long

211

period of thoughtful silence, then dug in a trouser pocket and placed a silver cartwheel on the bar top. "I'll bet either one of you, or both of you, he'll take her buggy ridin' within the next couple of days."

Rusty would not bet, but dour McGregor slapped down a silver dollar. "You hold the stakes," he told the saloonman, and frowned at his old friend. "You're tryin' to make out they're gettin' sweet on each other, an' as usual you're wrong as hell. Now I got work to do up at the shop. I can't stand around here jawbonin' all day . . . Rusty, you mind that bettin' money."

We hope that you enjoyed reading this
Sagebrush Large Print Western.
If you would like to read more Sagebrush titles,
ask your librarian or contact the Publishers:

United States and Canada

Thomas T. Beeler, *Publisher*
Post Office Box 659
Hampton Falls, New Hampshire 03844-0659
(800) 818-7574

United Kingdom, Eire, and
the Republic of South Africa

Isis Publishing Ltd
7 Centremead
Osney Mead
Oxford OX2 0ES England
(01865) 250333

Australia and New Zealand

Bolinda Publishing Pty. Ltd.
17 Mohr Street
Tullamarine, 3043, Victoria, Australia
(016103) 9338 0666